Something about this woman tugged at him.

Trey began to understand that she stirred up that long-buried yearning in him for a woman of his own. A family of his own.

Might as well get t̶ head. Laurie Oli , a life to return t

Besides the looking and he felt a ction to her, he figured his bi em was proximity. She was here, in his home, sharing his daily life.

But he knew better than to hit on her. She was his employee. She trusted him to treat her with respect. And that meant hands off.

But he wished, desperately, that when he looked at her again, he hadn't caught her staring at him with a look of curiosity in her eyes, a telltale blush staining her cheeks.

Dear Reader,

Around this time of year, everyone reflects on what it is that they're thankful for. For reader favorite Susan Mallery, the friendships she's made since becoming a writer have made a difference in her life. Bestselling author Sherryl Woods is thankful for the letters from readers—"It means so much to know that a particular story has touched someone's soul." And popular author Janis Reams Hudson is thankful "for the readers who spend their hard-earned money to buy my books."

I'm thankful to have such a talented group of writers in the Silhouette Special Edition line, and the authors appearing this month are no exception! In *Wrangling the Redhead* by Sherryl Woods, find out if the heroine's celebrity status gets in the way of true love.... Also don't miss *The Sheik and the Runaway Princess* by Susan Mallery, in which the Prince of Thieves kidnaps a princess…and simultaneously steals her heart!

When the heroine claims her late sister's child, she finds the child's guardian—and possibly the perfect man—in *Baby Be Mine* by Victoria Pade. And when a handsome horse breeder turns out to be a spy enlisted to expose the next heiress to the Haskell fortune, will he find an impostor or the real McCoy in *The Missing Heir* by Jane Toombs? In Ann Roth's *Father of the Year,* should this single dad keep his new nanny…or make her his wife? And the sparks fly when a man discovers his secret baby daughter left on his doorstep…which leads to a marriage of convenience in Janis Reams Hudson's *Daughter on His Doorstep.*

I hope you enjoy all these wonderful novels by some of the most talented authors in the genre. Best wishes to you and your family for a very happy and healthy Thanksgiving!

Best,

Karen Taylor Richman
Senior Editor

Please address questions and book requests to:
Silhouette Reader Service
U.S.: 3010 Walden Ave., P.O. Box 1325, Buffalo, NY 14269
Canadian: P.O. Box 609, Fort Erie, Ont. L2A 5X3

Daughter on His Doorstep

JANIS REAMS HUDSON

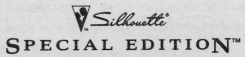

SPECIAL EDITION™

Published by Silhouette Books

America's Publisher of Contemporary Romance

This one's for Lynn, who, with one daughter already,
took on another man's two children when he remarried,
and made them his own. When we called him our
stepfather, I hope people understood the love that
went with that word. He was, quite simply, the best.

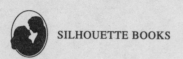 SILHOUETTE BOOKS

ISBN 0-373-24434-7

DAUGHTER ON HIS DOORSTEP

Copyright © 2001 by Janis Reams Hudson

Books by Janis Reams Hudson

Silhouette Special Edition

Resist Me If You Can #1037
The Mother of His Son #1095
Ilis Daughter's Laughter #1105
Until You #1210
*Their Other Mother #1267
*The Price of Honor #1332
*A Child on the Way #1349
*Daughter on His Doorstep #1434

*Wilders of Wyatt County

JANIS REAMS HUDSON

was born in California, grew up in Colorado, lived in Texas for a few years and now calls central Oklahoma home. She is the author of more than twenty-five novels, both contemporary and historical romances. Her books have appeared on the Waldenbooks, B. Dalton and Bookrack bestseller lists and earned numerous awards, including the National Readers' Choice Award and Reviewer's Choice awards from *Romantic Times Magazine*. She is a three-time finalist for the coveted RITA Award from Romance Writers of America and is a past president of RWA.

THE WILDERS

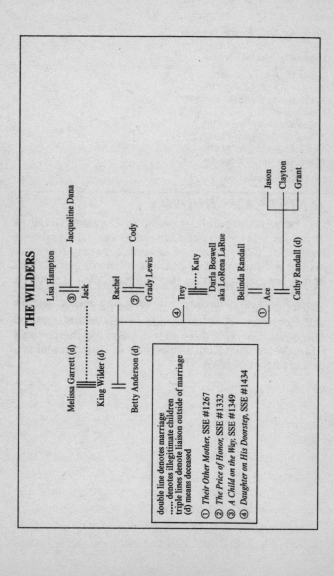

Melissa Garrett (d)
King Wilder (d)

Lisa Hampton
③
Jack

Jacqueline Dana

Betty Anderson (d)

Rachel
②
Grady Lewis

Cody

Trey
④
Katy
Darla Boswell
aka LoRena LaRue

Belinda Randall

Ace
①
Cathy Randall (d)

Jason
Clayton
Grant

double line denotes marriage
..... denotes illegitimate children
triple lines denote liaison outside of marriage
(d) means deceased

① *Their Other Mother*, SSE #1267
② *The Price of Honor*, SSE #1332
③ *A Child on the Way*, SSE #1349
④ *Daughter on His Doorstep*, SSE #1434

Chapter One

One minute Trey Wilder was minding his own business, the next someone was thrusting a tiny bundle into his arms and throwing around words that numbed his brain. Words like *baby* and *girl* and *yours* and *daddy*.

The man before him was a lawyer pushing forty. The woman, a nurse, appeared to be in her midfifties. The baby's name, they said, was Katy, the product of a weekend Trey had supposedly spent with one Darla Boswell.

He'd been out standing in the middle of his alfalfa field—okay, so it was the family joke: was he out, standing in his field, or was he outstanding in his field?—waiting for the feeling of satisfaction to fill him at the sight of one of the best stands of alfalfa the Flying Ace Ranch had produced in years. Nature had been generous this spring, and Trey's crop management and irrigation strategies had been right on target. The first cutting was now dried, baled and stored for winter feed. If the remaining two cuttings of the season produced as expected, they'd get five tons per acre this year, more than enough to see the herd through winter.

But the feeling of satisfaction didn't fill him the way it should, the way it used to. Something was missing from Trey's life, and he wasn't sure what it was. It was all mixed up in his head. One minute he loved the free and easy single life he led, the next he was looking at all the kids his brothers and sister were having, the love they had each found with that one special mate, and sometimes he felt as if life was passing him by.

Which was ridiculous. He led a full life, a useful life. Without the crops he raised, the ranch that had been in his family for four generations now, with number five coming on fast, would wither and die. He was the farmer of the family.

Maybe that was it, he thought as he'd watched the gleaming new sedan creep down the road to avoid bottoming out in the ruts.

Time to haul out the box blade, he thought, and knock the top off the ruts again.

His brothers were ranchers. Cattlemen. His sister served the ranching community as a veterinarian. And here he was, out standing in his field.

But he liked farming, always had, even though he was perfectly at home on horseback, working cattle with the rest of them.

No, it wasn't the farming that had him dissatisfied. It was probably the fact that he was staring the big three-oh in the face on his next birthday. Turning thirty was enough to depress any man, he thought as the sedan stopped beside his mailbox at the end of his gravel drive, then turned in.

With long strides, Trey crossed through his alfalfa, stirring up the sweet fragrance as he went, and decided he ought to count his blessings. Many a man would envy the life he led. He answered to no one, except, of course, Mother Nature and God, both of whom exhibited a sharp sense of humor by keeping him in check whenever he got too cocky. Like when he started counting his bales before they were stacked.

He'd never seen the car before, nor the stranger who stepped out of it wearing an expensive three-piece suit and looking as out of place on Trey's dusty drive as champagne at a beer bust.

Lost. That was Trey's thought. The man was probably looking for the Kovic place, another two miles west. Visitors to Wyatt County had a hard time realizing how far it was from one place to the next out here in the middle of Wyoming.

"Hi," Trey offered, noting that the woman in the back seat was unharnessing a baby from one of those car seat carryall things they strapped babies into. His brother Jack had one just like it for his and Lisa's baby girl. "Can I help you?"

The man stuck out his hand. "I'm Robert Stover. I'm looking for Trey Wilder."

"You've found him," Trey said, accepting the man's handshake. "What can I do for you?"

The stranger named Stover smiled. "It's what we've come to do for you. Or rather, to give you."

That's when it happened. The man turned and nodded toward the gray-haired woman in the car, and she got out carrying the baby, which she proceeded to plop into Trey's arms. Just plopped it there. Right there in his arms before Trey realized what was happening.

"Katy," the woman said to the infant, "this is your daddy."

Trey gaped at the woman. The man. The baby. The man again. "No way!"

A pained look came over the man's face. "I take it Ms. Boswell did not call you."

The baby squirmed in Trey's arms. "Who?"

"Katy's mother. Darla Boswell."

"There, that proves it. You've got the wrong man." Trey tried to return the baby to the woman, but she backed away and shook her head.

"I believe," the man said, "that you knew her by her stage name, LoRena LaRue."

Something that felt like a red-hot lead ball—big and heavy and burning—dropped to the pit of Trey's stomach.

Oh, jeez, oh damn. LoRena LaRue of the flaming red hair and teasing brown eyes, the talented mouth and the mile-long dancer's legs. LoRena LaRue of the wild Las Vegas weekend just…Trey gulped. Just a little more than nine months ago. LoRena LaRue, who, after their torrid weekend together, had cried on his shoulder because she had finally realized she was still in love with her old flame.

Trey stared down at the baby in his arms. The baby had enough thick, black hair, and eyes so blue, that she was a dead ringer for every baby the Wilders had managed to produce in at least the last two generations.

"I see that name rings a bell," the man said mildly.

"I told you she wouldn't call him," said the woman beside Stover.

"My apologies," Stover said. "My client—"

"Client?" Trey figured it was too much to hope that the man was LoRena's accountant.

"I'm Ms. Boswell's attorney. She was supposed to call you about Katy and tell you we were coming."

"Tell me?" Trey looked at the man, bewildered. Terrified.

"She was afraid you would say no," the woman added.

"No? No to what? You can't— She doesn't think— Good God, she really thinks this baby is *mine?*"

Robert Stover smiled in sympathy. "I realize this is a shock, Mr. Wilder. I'll be glad to explain everything."

"Perhaps we could go inside?" the woman suggested. "All this dust and sun isn't good for the baby."

Trey Wilder was a big man, six feet tall, a hard-muscled 190 pounds. He had a college degree and a good brain to go with it. He'd grown-up tough, with a father who didn't believe in softness of any kind in a man or a boy. Trey had done his share of bronc riding, steer wrestling and other foolishly dangerous stunts. When he was eight he'd broken his arm and hadn't shed so much as a tear over the pain.

He was afraid of nothing, took no lip from anyone. But just then he could do no more than stare at these people, their outlandish words buzzing around in his head like angry bees ready to swarm. The tiny bundle in his arms had short-circuited his brain. Somehow he found himself a moment later carrying her as he ushered the man and woman into his home.

In his living room he looked around, seeing nothing, imagining that this was what being shell-shocked felt like.

The tiny bundle in his arms chose that moment to let out a mewling little whimper. Worried that he might be squeezing her too hard, Trey looked down…and lost his heart.

"There, there, sweetheart, I'm sorry." Holding her awkwardly, afraid he was doing it wrong, he tried patting her gently. "I didn't mean to hold you so tight. It's just that these folks here kinda took me by surprise, is all. They think I'm your daddy, but it's all some big mistake."

The infant girl stared right at him, as though fascinated by his every word.

"We'll get it all straightened out in no time and get you on your way to wherever it is you belong. You are a sweetheart, aren't you?"

Trey glanced up then, ready to hand the baby back, because obviously there'd been a big mistake here.

Both the woman and the attorney—what had he said his name was? Stover. Robert Stover—were headed back outside.

"Hey," Trey protested. "Where—"

But there was no one in the room to answer. No one but a tiny angel named Katy, and she wasn't talking.

Trey was so stunned that all he could do was stand there and stare at her. Was she his? Was this beautiful baby from him? Could he and the alluring LoRena LaRue have created this miracle?

He must have been in a daze—maybe even in shock—because when he looked up again from those giant blue eyes, his living room was filled with baby paraphernalia. Stacks of disposable diaper packages, cartons of formula, boxes of clothes, a pile of baby-care books, and against the far wall, Stover and the woman were setting up a portable crib.

A new sense of alarm snaked up Trey's spine. "Now, wait just a minute. You can't mean to leave her here," he cried.

Stover straightened and turned to face Trey. "That's entirely up to you, of course. But as you're the baby's father, I'm not sure you'll care for the alternative."

More suspicious than ever, Trey narrowed his eyes. "I don't think I like the sound of that. What alternative? Where's LoRena? Why didn't she come? Why did she send you?"

Stover dusted off his hands and frowned. "This would have been so much easier on everyone if she'd called you, as she said she would."

The baby began squirming in Trey's arms, so he jiggled her a little. "What was she supposed to tell me? Why didn't she tell me she was pregnant?"

"Because she feared you were the type of man who would insist on marrying her to give the baby your name."

"Well, of course I would," Trey proclaimed.

"Which is exactly what she did not want. The marriage part, at least. To put it bluntly, Mr. Wilder, Ms. Boswell never had any intention of raising a child. She had arranged for the baby to be adopted."

"Without even telling me I was about to become a father?"

"That's right."

"Why, that—"

"But the adoption fell through at the last minute. If you don't want to raise your daughter yourself, I'm instructed to take the baby back to Nevada and turn her over to the state for them to put up for adoption."

"The hell you will," Trey said without thought. "Wilder babies aren't raised by strangers. In this family we take care of our own."

Stover smiled. "That's what she thought you would say."

An hour later Attorney Stover and Nurse Nancy— imagine someone named Nancy becoming a nurse and not appreciating the joke—drove away. They had answered all his questions about how and why. He was left with *What now?*

He stood beside the crib and looked at the tiny angel sleeping there. If she wasn't his daughter, he was in big trouble, because he was already head-over-heels in love with young Katy.

But he really didn't doubt that she was his. He

would have the tests done to eliminate any question, but that would be just to satisfy his family and the law. Just the law, really. His family would accept her, if he did. But he already knew the truth, felt it in his gut. This child was his daughter.

What he didn't know was how he was going to take care of her. He didn't suppose he could just strap her to his back every morning and head out to the fields or the pastures or the range to work. He was going to need help, and plenty of it.

I'm a father.

The thought still shocked him. Thrilled him. Terrified him.

The baby opened her eyes, kicked her feet and cried.

"Uh-oh. Hey, baby girl," he said as he picked her up carefully, holding her head the way Nurse Nancy had told him, the way he'd seen his brothers hold their babies. The way he'd held them himself more than a few times, but that was different. The other babies hadn't been his. "You hungry, sweetheart?"

Hmm. How was he supposed to fix her bottle while holding her?

He put her back down in the crib. Before he'd gone two feet she let out what he considered a very unlady-like howl.

As if he were a yo-yo and she had her little hand through the loop at the end of the string, he bolted back to her side. "Come on, now, sweet pea. Ah, hell, your diaper? Again?"

Okay, he could do this. Nurse Nancy had made him

do it three times before she and Stover left. He could handle it. Of course he could handle it.

By the time he was finished, he had to admit that it didn't look as neat as the last one, but he figured it would do. Katy had stopped crying. That was good enough for Trey.

He stood over the crib and stared down at...his daughter. God above, he had a daughter.

What was he supposed to do now? How was he supposed to raise a baby alone and run the farm and help out at the ranch?

As if she believed he was blaming her for causing all this turmoil, little Katy scrunched up her face and started crying. Pitifully.

"Food," Trey said desperately. "Maybe she needs to be fed again. Is that it, sweet pea? Are you hungry now? You just wait right here and I'll fix you a bottle." If he remembered how.

Nancy had shown him how to fit the pouch of formula into the nurser. She'd shown him a lot of things in such a short time; he was sure he'd already forgotten half of them.

What was it she'd said to him with that smug look on her face when she'd been showing him the baby books and the pile of typewritten instructions she'd prepared for him? Something about, "I know it goes against your genetic code, but you simply *must* read this material. It's full of instructions you're going to need."

Okay, great. It was about time babies started coming with instructions. But the little booger was really tuning up now, and she looked so miserable that Trey wanted to cry right along with her. He couldn't bear to leave her alone in her crib while he went to the kitchen and heated a bottle. She would think he had abandoned her.

He got the carrier/car seat thing, put her in and carried her with him to the kitchen.

Instructions be damned. Any idiot could put a pouch of formula into a nurser and heat it up. He placed it in the microwave just as Katy tuned up and started wailing again.

"Ah, come on, sweet pea." He punched numbers and started the microwave, then turned away instantly and picked up the baby. "I'm hurrying, honest I am."

Young Katy was not impressed. Her eyes scrunched shut and leaked tears, while her mouth opened wide with a pitiful cry.

"Give a guy a break, huh? I'm new at this."

A new thought struck him. Still holding Katy, he turned and glared at the microwave. What if the nut-cases were right? What if microwaves really did put deadly rays in the food?

He swore.

As if to let him know exactly what she thought of his cussing, Katy made a terrible face and filled her diaper with some of the most foul-smelling stuff it had ever been Trey's displeasure to encounter. Then she screamed louder.

He laid her on the table and tried to get the diaper off, but Katy's little legs slipped from his grasp and she plopped right back down into the stinking mess in her diaper, getting it all over herself and splattering some onto his shirt.

Trey stared down at himself, stunned. One small

blob of baby poop rolled off his shirt and landed on the toe of his boot.

The phone started ringing.

Katy cried harder.

The formula pouch in the microwave exploded.

Help!

It was only Monday.

Chapter Two

Salt Lake City, Utah

Heaven help her, it was only June. Laurie Oliver didn't see how she was going to survive the rest of the summer living with her parents. At least, not with her sanity intact.

The wall between the living room and the front bedroom vibrated to the deep bass beat of her youngest brother's stereo. The opposite wall, separating the living room from the single-car garage, shook in time with the shouting match going on in the garage between Laurie's parents.

On the sofa, Laurie's youngest daughter, five-year-old Amy, huddled in on herself in defense against hearing her grandparents go at each other. Next to her, Amy's six-year-old sister, Carrie, wasn't quite as sensitive about the argument in the garage as she was mad at her uncle Billy's rudeness in turning up his stereo. With a mutinous expression on her normally serene face, Carrie held out the TV remote and pressed the up arrow on the volume control.

Laurie and the girls had been at her parents' house barely a week, and it had been the same scene every day. Pouting brother, fighting parents. She was only grateful that the girls were asleep when David, her other brother, came in late every night reeking of whisky.

Laurie closed her eyes and prayed for patience. If it hadn't rained all morning, leaving the backyard a boggy mess, she could send the girls outside to play. Having a yard to play in was a new concept to them; they would have enjoyed themselves. But it was too close to dinner, and Carrie detested mud, so that particular diversion was out.

The good news was there was only one more week left in June. Then it would be July, then August, and she and her girls would be leaving. If she didn't commit murder in the meantime.

Squaring her shoulders, Laurie marched to her brothers' bedroom door and knocked.

When they were kids, Laurie had had a room to herself, while Billy and David had shared. When Laurie married and moved out, Billy had taken over her old room. Now, with her and the girls moving in for the summer, Billy had been forced to move back in with David, and neither of her brothers were happy about it.

Laurie might have felt a twinge more guilt over

disrupting the household, except that everyone was acting like such snots about being inconvenienced. She just couldn't find any more guilt in her. Billy was acting like a pouty two-year-old.

She knocked again on the bedroom door.

Naturally, Billy wouldn't have heard a dozen stampeding buffalo outside his door, his music was so loud, so Laurie got no response.

This time she pounded. When that got her nothing, she turned the knob and pushed the door open.

Her eighteen-year-old brother, Lord love him, lay sprawled on his back on his bed, sound asleep. Until she hit the off button on his stereo.

Billy popped straight up and blinked. "Hey." His protest came from a scratchy-sounding throat. "Leave that alone. I was listening to it."

"You were asleep, and it was so loud the girls couldn't hear the television in the living room. After I asked you twice to turn it down."

"I don't see what the big deal is." He sneered as only a put-upon eighteen-year-old could. "Besides, you're not the boss of me."

Laurie resisted the urge to bang her head against the wall. She didn't figure the poor wall could take any more trauma after being blasted with hard rock music for the better part of the day. Besides, it wouldn't get her anything but a bruise. Instead, she prayed again for patience and sat on the edge of Billy's bed.

"Look," she said. "I'm sorry that my moving back home for the summer has put you out of your room. I know you don't want to share with David again, but you're doing it anyway, and I love you for it."

Billy stared at the ceiling, completely unimpressed.

Laurie fought the urge to shake him. "This isn't all fun and games for me, either, you know."

"Yeah, sure."

"You think I like moving back here and sharing a room and a bed with both of my daughters? You think I like having my eardrums assaulted day and night with your music? You think I like hearing Mom and Dad go at each other all the time?"

"So move out. It's not my fault you couldn't keep a husband."

The pain of Billy's barb surprised her with its sharpness. Mostly, she thought, hoped, because her little brother knew it would hurt and said it anyway. That the little boy she'd loved and coddled all his life would be so intentionally cruel sliced deep.

"You've gotten mean," she managed.

Flushed, Billy had the good grace to look away. "Sorry," he mumbled.

"You should be. It was a cheap shot. Besides, what makes you think I wanted to keep him?"

Billy looked at her and cocked his head, interest lighting his eyes. "Why wouldn't you? I thought that's what all women wanted, a husband."

"Not when he's immature, irresponsible and unfaithful." She had to admit that that last one still hurt. She knew she wasn't to blame for Jimmy's immaturity or his inability to accept responsibility for his own actions, but had she somehow driven him into the arms of another woman?

No. She'd been over and over it. She was not responsible for Jimmy's behavior. Not any more so than she was for her apartment owner's decision to sell the complex she'd lived in for five years to a developer who planned to level it and put up a parking garage, forcing her and everyone else to move right at the start of summer.

"Jimmy was a jerk," Billy said.

"He was," Laurie agreed. "But I won't have you saying that or anything else bad about him around the girls. He's still their father and they love him, and that's as it should be."

Billy's only response was a shrug.

"I'll have your word on that," she said.

He gave her another shrug.

"I mean it, Billy. Your word."

"Yeah, yeah."

She would have pressed the point further, but she heard the phone ring in the kitchen. She preferred to answer it herself before one of the girls got it. The last time Amy answered the phone, she had ordered seven magazines before Laurie got there.

It wasn't a magazine salesman this time. Laurie felt relief and pleasure at hearing the voice of her father's sister. Aunt Donna was the one sane and steady member of the entire family. "How are you? How is Wyoming?"

"I'm fine. Wyoming's fine. How are things there?"

"Don't ask," Laurie said, unwilling to even think about the tension and unhappiness in the house, now that she was talking with one of her very favorite people. "What's that I hear in the background? It sounds like a baby."

Donna chuckled. "That's little Katy, our newest Wilder."

For the past couple of years Donna had worked on a ranch, the Flying Ace, somewhere in southwestern Wyoming. The ranch was owned by the three Wilder brothers and their sister; Donna served as housekeeper and nanny for the oldest brother and his wife and children. Aunt Donna always had a funny story to tell about one Wilder or another. Laurie had heard so much about them since Donna had gone to work for them that she felt as if she knew them herself. "The Wilders have a new baby?"

"And what a little sweetheart she is," Donna said.

Laurie could hear the smile in her aunt's voice. "How old is she? I don't remember you mentioning your boss was expecting."

"She wasn't. This is Trey's baby."

"Trey? He's the youngest brother, right?"

"You've got a good memory."

"It's easy. There's Ace, then Jack, then Trey. And Rachel, of course."

"That's them, all right."

"Wasn't Trey the carefree bachelor of the family? I don't remember you saying anything about him getting married."

"Well," Donna said, drawing the word out. "No, I didn't, because he didn't. But he's got himself the prettiest little baby girl you ever did see. Next to you, when you were born, that is. And your babies."

"Ah." Laurie laughed. "Nice save. So, since Trey doesn't have a wife, does this mean you're taking care of the baby for him? How is that working out?"

Donna sighed loudly enough for Laurie to hear it plainly over the phone. "It's not working out well. At least not for Trey. And frankly, we're all running out of steam around here, what with spring roundup and Ace's three hellions out of school for the summer and now the baby. Trey's been trying to hire somebody to live in at his place and take care of Katy for him, but so far no takers."

"Why can't he just leave her with you during the day? Or is that not workable?"

"It could work," Donna said. "In fact it's working now. But Trey feels as though he's asking too much of me and the family. He's determined to raise this baby, and he wants her raised in his home. Plus, even when he leaves her here with us all day, he doesn't get much sleep when he takes her home at night. He needs help at home."

Laurie smiled. "Too bad he doesn't live around here. I might take the job myself. It would be nice to hold a baby again."

Donna chuckled in sympathy. "Are your girls growing up on you?"

"Yes. Too fast. Anyway, I wish him luck. And you, too, until he hires someone. Do you want to talk to Dad?"

"Are he and your mother still…"

"Raising the roof? Yes," Laurie said darkly. "I'm surprised you can't hear them."

"All I hear is the television."

"That's the girls. They have to turn it up full-blast to hear it over Billy's stereo and Mom and Dad's yelling."

"Oh, good grief," Donna said with disgust. "That's ridiculous."

"You're telling me. If I had the money and a place, I'd get the girls out of here in a hurry."

"Oh, honey, is it that bad?"

"Aunt Donna, I've never seen the family like this before. I think our staying here is only making things worse, and I don't know what to do about it."

"When is your house supposed to be ready for you to move into?"

Laurie closed her eyes and brought a picture to mind. Her house. Fresh white paint, dark-green trim, lots of sparkling windows. It would be her first home of her own. The first house her daughters would ever have lived in. No thin apartment walls with noisy neighbors on the other side. No clomping footsteps overhead at all hours of the day and night. A nice fenced yard instead of a concrete parking lot. And located less than two blocks from the school the girls were going to attend and where Laurie would start her new teaching job in the fall.

Oh, she couldn't wait.

"The middle of August," she told Donna. "That's when the seller's new house is scheduled to be finished so they can move."

"Are you counting the days?"

"I'm counting the minutes. It'll be a miracle if I don't grab the girls and run away from this madhouse long before then."

"Well," Donna said, "if you get the urge, come on up here to the ranch. You can stay here at the main house and you and I can have a good visit. And I'll

get to spend time with my two beautiful grand-
nieces.''

For a minute, a short one, Laurie was more than
tempted. But reality and common sense reeled her in
quickly. ''Oh, Aunt Donna, don't think I wouldn't
love to see you. But we can't freeload on the Wilders.''

''What freeload? You're invited. They've been telling me since I came here that I'm free to have visitors
come stay with us.''

There came that temptation again, but Laurie resisted. It just wouldn't be right to live off her aunt's
employers.

''You think about it,'' Donna told her. ''You could
help us take care of sweet little Katy, and Carrie and
Amy could learn to ride horses.''

''I think I'd better go now,'' Laurie said with a
laugh. ''Before I give in when I know I shouldn't.
Here comes Dad. Do you want to talk to him?''

''As a matter-of-fact, I do. Put him on.''

When Donna Harris hung up the phone, she was
shaking her head. ''Where did I go wrong?''

Her employer and friend, Belinda Wilder, shifted
little Katy on her shoulder. To the baby she said,
''There, there, sweetheart.'' To Donna she asked,
''Problems back home?''

Donna shook her head again, at herself. ''Somewhere during the course of taking care of my four
younger brothers after Mama died, I managed to let
at least one of them, Tom, turn out to be an imbecile.''

"If he's an imbecile, I doubt that's your fault," Belinda said, swaying back and forth because the motion quieted the baby.

"You're right. I raised him better than that. I raised all of them better than that. But right now I want to pinch Tom's head off and tell the good Lord he died."

"That bad, huh?" Belinda asked.

Because they were more than employer and employee—in fact, they were close friends—Donna told Belinda about the situation at Tom's house. About the arguments between Tom and his wife, Susan, about Billy's belligerence and David's drinking. About Laurie and her daughters being forced to move back in with them because her apartment complex was being torn down.

"Poor girl's divorce hasn't been final hardly more than a year. By the way, that jerk of an ex of hers forgot how to make out a child support check months ago. Now she's lost her apartment and can't find another one because prices for everything in Salt Lake City have gone sky high because of the Olympics, and she has to put up with idiots at home. The tension is so tight in that house you could bounce a quarter off it. It's the last thing Laurie and her daughters need."

Belinda continued walking the baby around the kitchen while Donna started dinner. "What's she going to do?" Belinda asked. "It doesn't sound like she's going to want to stay there for long."

"I guess she's going to grit her teeth and wait for her house to be ready in August."

"Why don't you invite her up here?"

Donna paused with a potato in one hand and a peeler in the other. "I did."

"Good."

"She turned me down. Thinks she'd be freeloading off my employers."

"Well, that's just nonsense," Belinda said.

Donna smiled and started peeling the potato in her hand. She dearly loved Belinda Wilder, she surely did. All the Wilders, in fact. "I told her that," she said. "But she's got her fair share of pride."

"Maybe if you give her a few days and ask again, she might change her mind."

Considering the atmosphere in Tom and Susan's house, Donna thought that might be a distinct possibility.

After Donna's phone call that night, things changed in the Harris household. Whatever Donna said to Laurie's father had an immediate effect. The yelling stopped at once.

That wasn't to say that the tension eased or the atmosphere lightened, but suddenly Laurie's parents were all smiles. As long as you didn't catch one of them looking at the other when they thought no one was watching.

Despite the change, Laurie and her daughters were more miserable by the day. There was no help for it: Laurie was going to have to try to find a summer job. If she couldn't find an affordable place to rent, at least she could pay for day care and get Carrie and Amy out of the house for a few hours each day.

A sad state of affairs, indeed, when day care became preferable to grandparents.

After spending the most ho-hum Fourth of July imaginable—at least her daughters had enjoyed the commercial fireworks extravaganza—Laurie knew she couldn't put it off any longer. The next morning after breakfast, while the girls were watching cartoons, Laurie snatched that morning's edition of the *Salt Lake Tribune* and a cup of coffee and settled at the kitchen table to peruse the classifieds.

The paper was not helpful. By her second cup of coffee she knew she was going to have to go to the unemployment office or drive to the area fast-food restaurants and look for Help Wanted signs in the windows.

So much for earning enough to be able to afford a place to live until her house was available. She would barely be able to afford day care for the girls on fast-food wages.

The phone rang, interrupting her downwardly spiraling thoughts.

It was Donna. "How serious were you the last time we talked when you said you were ready to run away from home?"

"Serious enough that I'm sitting here reading the want ads as we speak."

"Looking for a job?" Donna asked.

"Looking," Laurie admitted. "But not finding."

"Good. We need you up here."

"Pardon?"

"We've got the chicken pox."

Laurie frowned. "Chicken pox?"

"Yeah, you know, little red bumps that itch like crazy and jump from one kid to the next in the blink of an eye."

"Very funny," Laurie said. "Aren't you a little old to be catching them?"

"Now who's funny?" Donna said. "*I* don't have the chicken pox, Clay does."

"Clay's the middle boy, right?"

"That's right. He's six. And he's miserable, and it's only a matter of time before Jason and Grant both come down with chicken pox. And that's why we need you."

"You need help taking care of them?" Laurie said carefully. If Donna needed her, Laurie would go, certainly. Carrie and Amy had been vaccinated against chicken pox, so it wasn't likely they would get sick.

"Not the boys," Donna said. "Belinda and I can handle them. But Trey won't bring the baby here as long as the boys have something contagious, and Lisa can't keep her during the day because she broke her leg two days ago and it's all she can do to keep up with her own baby."

"It sounds as if you've really got your hands full. Just what is it you want me to do?"

"Trey wants to hire you as his temporary live in nanny/housekeeper while he searches for someone permanent."

"Oh, Donna, I don't know…"

"I'm sure you've got a few reservations about moving into a house with a man you've never met."

"It's not—"

"I don't blame you," Donna said. "But I'll tell

you that Trey Wilder is a good man, Laurie. He's fair and honest and is totally devoted to little Katy. He said your girls are welcome in his home, so don't think there's any problem there. And did I mention that the pay is excellent?''

Laurie felt the phone slip; her palm had grown damp. Heavens, her pulse was racing at the mere thought of spending a few weeks on a job in Wyoming. Whether it was nerves, excitement or fear, she didn't know. It was probably doubt. Laurie had never been a spur-of-the-moment type of person. She didn't just jump up and do something, not without giving it sufficient thought. She would need to mull over this job offer, test it out in her mind. Sleep on it a day or two. But she needed all the information she could get—such as the salary.

''How excellent?'' she asked her aunt.

The amount Donna quoted made Laurie's eyes bulge. It wasn't a fortune, to be sure, but it was a darn sight more than she would make at a fast-food job and even more than she could make teaching for the same length of time.

The most amazing words came out of her mouth. ''When does he want me to start?''

With his six-week-old daughter strapped to his chest in a blue canvas sling, Trey Wilder took another look around his kitchen.

''What do you think, sweet pea?'' He gently patted Katy's back. ''Think it'll do? We don't want her to think we're a couple of slobs.''

It was probably ridiculous to be so nervous about

finally hiring a live-in housekeeper/nanny. Okay, definitely ridiculous. But he would be trusting Katy to this stranger, even if it was only temporary, until he could find someone permanent.

Sure, he wanted the woman to like him, to adore Katy. But he ought to be worrying about whether or not he was going to like her.

Of course, she *was* Donna's niece, so she had to be likable. And she had two young daughters, so that meant she knew how to take care of a baby. Having two little girls around would give Trey good experience for when Katy was older, too.

Katy squirmed against his chest and let out a whimper.

Trey smoothed a hand along her back. "It'll be fine, sweet pea. We trust Donna." And he did trust Donna, implicitly. He figured he was just anxious for the woman to get here so he could meet her and decide for himself if he would be able to tolerate sharing his home with her. And her daughters.

Three ladies were moving in with him this afternoon—with him, Trey Wilder, who hadn't shared a home with anyone since he'd built this house for himself nearly ten years ago. Now it was going to be overrun with females.

He couldn't believe how much his life had changed in the three weeks since Katy came to live with him. Couldn't believe how much he had changed. His outlook, his priorities. His heart. The latter had been stolen, no doubt about it.

He looked down at the child strapped to his chest. "What do you think, sweet pea, are you worth it?"

Katy's tiny face scrunched up in a frown.

"Hey there, girl." Trey placed a small kiss on the top of her head. "You know I was only kidding. I wouldn't trade you for anything." He closed his eyes and brushed his cheek over her fine, dark hair. "Not anything. And if we don't like this lady, we'll just send her packing. Deal?"

Katy gave a tiny little baby sigh against his chest.

Trey smiled. "Good. Now that we've got that settled, we've got time for a walk before they get here. What say we go be out standing in our field?"

At the entrance to the Flying Ace Ranch Laurie pulled her car to the side of the road and stopped. They'd been on the road for four hours, two hundred miles, one mediocre lunch and six bathroom stops. And their trip was almost over.

It was crazy, taking a job from a man she'd never even spoken with. It had to be crazy. But there had been no time. Trey Wilder had asked Donna to handle the hiring, as he was out on some emergency until late last night.

Good heavens, Donna had offered her the job only yesterday, and here she was, hauling her daughters to a stranger's house, where they would live for the next several weeks.

She had to be out of her mind, because she was actually excited about the whole idea. Not the stranger part, but she looked forward to taking care of a baby again, and a house. All Laurie had ever wanted to be was a good mother and homemaker. It had been her dream for years.

But she was a practical person, so she'd gone to college and gotten her teaching degree. That had saved her after the divorce when she'd become the sole supporter of herself and her daughters. She knew she would always need to work for wages now, but this one last shot at her dream, at making a home, caring for another baby...

"Are we there?"

Laurie gave herself a mental shake. That was the fifth time in the past two hours that one of the girls had asked that question. At least this time Laurie didn't have to say no. Not exactly, anyway.

"Almost," she told them, unfastening her seat belt so she could turn toward the back seat. "We're on the ranch. It's a few more miles to Mr. Wilder's house, so we need to comb our hair and straighten our clothes."

"So we'll look nice for our new boss," Amy stated.

Carrie rolled her eyes. "He's not *our* boss, silly, he's Mama's boss."

Because all mothers are contortionists, of necessity, Laurie twisted and leaned and reached, and within a few minutes had her daughters' hair and clothing as neat as possible under the circumstances. Then with another check of Donna's directions, which had her bypassing the ranch headquarters and going straight to Trey's house on the other side of the ranch to avoid the chicken pox, they were on their way, the final leg of their journey to what Laurie had told the girls was a grand adventure—living on a ranch.

Carrie and Amy, and Laurie, too, for that matter,

were city girls. They knew nothing of living in the
country, and country was all they'd seen for the past
four hours. Signs of civilization, such as towns, had
been few and far between.

Now, here, on the Wilders' Flying Ace, the only
signs of civilization Laurie could see were the gravel
road, the electric line strung between poles beside the
road, and mile after mile of barb wire fence. Aside
from those signs of man's presence, there was nothing
but flat land extending forever. Or at least to the
mountains in the west.

Of course, living in Salt Lake City, Laurie and her
girls were no strangers to flat, empty land. There was
no flatter nor emptier land on earth than the Great
Salt Desert that stretched westward from the city.

"When will we get there, Mama?" Amy whined.

Poor little girl, Laurie thought, pulling her mind
back to the business at hand. *Girls,* she amended.
Both of them had been strapped into the back seat for
hours. They needed to get out and play.

"Mama?" The whine now bordered on a demand.

"We only have a few more miles," Laurie said,
putting the car in gear and pulling back onto the
gravel road. "It won't be long."

"That's what you said last time," Amy muttered.

But this time it truly wasn't long, although the
word *long* was a relative term. To a five-year-old *long*
could be three minutes. The last twenty minutes of
their drive probably rated *eternity* to Amy.

Finally, Laurie spotted the mailbox Donna had de-
scribed and, next to it, Trey Wilder's driveway. Be-

side the driveway sat a white pickup with a red-and-black Flying Ace Ranch logo on the driver's door.

A long, wide porch stretched the length of a neat, single-story white frame house. The shutters and trim were a deep, forest green, giving it a clean, tidy appearance.

Off to the west about fifty yards stood a huge barn and several other smaller buildings and, beyond them, long, wide fields of some type of grass or hay. What Laurie knew about crops was so little as to be laughable.

She drove slowly up the driveway and parked beside the pickup. She was reaching for the key to turn off the engine when a tall, black-haired man with a baby strapped to his chest stepped around the corner of the garage.

This, she thought, must be Trey Wilder.

My, oh, my. Laurie couldn't remember the last time the mere sight of a man had tripped her pulse—couldn't remember the last time *anything* had tripped her pulse, if she was honest. Something about the way he moved—slowly, as though he had all the time in the world, yet with a deliberate purpose—gave her the impression that he knew exactly where he was going and would get there sooner rather than later.

Laurie wondered if he moved that slowly, that deliberately, in bed.

Good grief! She couldn't believe such a thought had popped into her head. *Down, girl.* Men were definitely not on her menu these days. She didn't have the time or the inclination. She had two daughters to raise, a new job to deal with, both now and at the end of summer when her teaching job started, and a life to rebuild.

For an instant, through the windshield of her car, Trey Wilder's eyes met hers, and she feared he could read every thought in her head. Never had she seen such piercingly brilliant blue eyes in her life.

Irritated with herself and her reaction to the man who was about to become her boss, she forced a smile and said over her shoulder, "We're here, girls."

Laurie was a bit slower and a great deal more sedate getting out of the car than were her daughters. By the time she removed the key from the ignition, retrieved her purse from the passenger seat, unhooked her seat belt and climbed out of the car, both girls were waiting for her. To their credit they did not approach the man and baby. Laurie was pleased that her lessons about strangers had, at least in this case, taken root.

The man approached, but stopped several feet away from her daughters. "Hello," he said to them. Then he looked up at Laurie again. "You'd be Laurie Oliver. I'm Trey Wilder. Welcome to the Flying Ace."

His voice was dark and smooth, like chocolate. Like black velvet. Like sin.

And I'm in trouble, Laurie thought. Then amusement—at herself—took over, and her smile was genuine as she stepped forward and held out her hand. "Thank you. We're glad to be here."

The unexpected jolt of electricity that shot up her arm when they shook hands made Laurie jerk.

Trey felt it, too, and narrowed his eyes to hide his reaction. Must be static electricity in the air, he decided. He'd never gotten a jolt from a woman merely by shaking her hand. And while this woman was particularly appealing—he'd always been a sucker for delicate blondes with big green eyes—she was here as his employee, to keep his house and care for his daughter. Not for him to pounce on.

He squatted down before her daughters and, as surreptitiously as possible, rubbed his hand along the thigh of his jeans to rid himself of the residual tingling sensation.

In his mind he quickly ran through the information Donna had given him. "You must be Miss Carrie Oliver," he said to the older of the two. He held out his hand to her. "How do you do?"

Her smile was tentative and fleeting. She gave him a small nod and barely touched his hand. "Very well, thank you."

A shy one, that. Not so her sister, if the gleam in the younger one's bright-green eyes—a slightly darker shade than her mother's—was anything to go on.

"And you," he said to her, "must be Miss Amy Oliver. Am I correct?"

The little one giggled and held out her hand for a shake. "That's me. Is that your baby?"

"Yes, ma'am, this is Miss Katy Wilder."

"She's a girl?" Amy asked.

"She sure is."

"Oh, good." Amy smiled. "That means she won't squirt you in the face when you change her diaper."

Trey mashed his lips together, fighting a hoot of

laughter, and looked everywhere but at the girl's mother.

"She's little," Amy went on. "Our cousin Jeffrey used to be a little baby, but that was a long time ago. He's a toppler now."

"No, silly." Carrie rolled her eyes at her sister. "It's *toddler,* not *toppler.*"

"S'not."

"S'too."

"Girls," their mother said darkly.

"He's a *toppler,*" Amy said fiercely. "That's why he keeps toppling over all the time. And I am not silly." She scrunched up her face but stopped when her mother spoke.

"Amy Oliver, don't you dare stick out your tongue. The two of you are going to have Mr. Wilder thinking I've raised a couple of ill-mannered hooligans."

Trey winked at the girls. To their mother he said, "I'm thinking you're raising a couple of typical kids."

"That's us." Amy grinned and held her hands out to her sides, palms up. "Jus' a couple of typical kids."

Trey decided it was time for a change of scene before he broke out laughing. "Come on inside," he invited. "I'll put Katy in her crib and bring in your things. I'm glad you could come on such short notice."

Trey ushered them into his home and showed them the bedrooms first. Laurie let the girls choose which of the two available rooms they wanted.

Thank God it was a four-bedroom house, Laurie

thought. She had been sharing a room—and a bed—with her daughters for weeks. She was more than ready for a little space and privacy, and she was sure the girls were, too.

Laurie left her daughters exploring their room and followed the sound of Trey's voice to the nursery.

"Oh, how wonderful." She turned in a circle to admire the teddy bears, balloons and butterflies painted in bold colors on the walls.

"Thanks," Trey said as he settled Katy in her crib. "The Wilder women did all this."

"Hmm." Laurie fought a grin. "Is that a group of your former lady loves, or your female relatives?"

Trey shook his head. "The family's gonna love you. But for the record, the Wilder women consist of Belinda, my brother Ace's wife...Lisa, my brother Jack's wife...my sister, Rachel, and your aunt Donna, whom we adopted years ago as a member of the tribe."

Laurie listened to him, but her gaze strayed to the baby in the crib. It had been a long time since she'd cared for a baby. "She's absolutely beautiful," she murmured.

"She is." Trey's voice softened. "She's perfect."

The two of them stood silently for a moment, watching as Katy stuck her fist in her mouth and drifted off to sleep.

Trey picked up the baby monitor and motioned toward the door. Out in the hall he said, "I'll go bring in your luggage then I'll show you the rest of the house."

Laurie helped him carry in their luggage, and en-

listed the girls to carry a few of their smaller belong-
ings.

While the girls started unpacking, Laurie left her
things for later and went to find Trey for her tour of
the house. She found him in the nursery, strapping
Katy to his chest again.

"She was awake," he said.

He gave Laurie the grand tour and showed her
where he kept the baby supplies, linens, cleaning supplies and everything in the kitchen.

Laurie had to admit, but only to herself, that she
had a little trouble concentrating on anything beyond
the sound of his deep, smooth voice. And that worried
her. It wasn't like her at all, so she told herself that
she'd just better get over it. She'd known the man
less than an hour and she was already fantasizing
about hearing that voice deep in the night, whispering
in her ear in the dark....

Good grief, where had that thought come from?

Wherever, it had just better get lost. There would
be no hanky-panky between her and her new boss.

"Is something wrong?"

Laurie blinked. "I'm sorry. What were you saying?
I'm afraid my mind wandered."

"That's okay," Trey said, wondering if perhaps
he'd made a mistake. She was sure pretty to look at,
but if she couldn't wrap her mind around the simple
things he was telling her, he wasn't sure he wanted
to leave her in charge of his daughter.

And when she did give him her full attention, she
looked at him oddly. As if she couldn't quite make
up her mind about something.

Well, that was fair, since he had yet to make up his mind about her.

Trey decided he would keep a close eye on this woman for the rest of the day and night. If he wasn't satisfied by morning that she could handle the job...well, he didn't know what the hell he would do, but he wouldn't leave Katy with her, that was for damn sure.

Chapter Three

"I haven't had time to stock up on groceries lately," Trey told Laurie when they reached the kitchen. "I've been eating over at Ace's when I go there to pick up Katy in the evenings. There's plenty of baby formula here, and in the garage there's a freezer full of beef, but not much to go with it."

"I'm sure I can put something together for tonight, but I'll need to shop tomorrow," Laurie told him.

"I've got a better idea. I know you're probably tired of being in a car, but why don't we drive to town, have supper at the café, then hit the grocery store? That way I can show you around town and help you get your bearings. I won't be able to do that tomorrow. Now that you're here I have to get back to work."

"Whatever you say," Laurie told him. "You're the boss."

Trey smiled at her. "If you're always this agreeable, you and I are going to get along fine."

"You mean, if I always agree with you?"

He laughed. "Well, it wouldn't hurt anything."

"Do you mind if I ask you a question?" Laurie asked.

"Ask away."

She tilted her head and, with a half smile, said, "Do you always carry the baby around like that?"

Trey looked down at Katy, still strapped to his chest, and frowned. "Like what? What's wrong with it?"

"Nothing," she said quickly, with a smile. "I've just never seen a man look so natural and easy wearing a slingful of baby. You move and act as though she's been strapped to you forever."

Trey's grin came slowly, but lacked nothing in wattage when it spread across his face. "I'll take that as a compliment."

"I meant it as one. For somebody who didn't even know he was about to become a father until the baby was handed to you, you're a natural. Most men wouldn't appear so comfortable." Jimmy certainly hadn't been. He still never knew quite how to act around his daughters.

"Then most men," Trey said, looking down at the baby with more love on his face than she'd ever seen on a man, "are fools. They don't know what they're missing."

Laurie's heart turned over in her chest. Oh, she

thought, she was really going to like working for a man who worshiped a baby that way.

A moment later Trey said, "So, I guess Donna told you all about us."

"You and Katy?"

"Yeah."

"I asked a lot of questions. A lone woman with two young daughters needs to be careful when she agrees to move into a man's house and live under the same roof with him."

"I guess when you put it that way, I see your point."

"Besides," Laurie added with a small smile. "I'm sure Donna told you everything there is to know about me."

He tilted his head and absently stroked Katy's back. "What makes you think so?"

"Because I don't think you'd let a stranger you knew nothing about anywhere near your daughter, much less have her live in and take care of her."

"You're right. I wouldn't."

"So we're even," Laurie said. "I'm here and ready to take care of Katy and your home, but if there's a certain way you want anything done, you'll have to tell me."

"We can go over all of that on the way into town. It's nearly an hour's drive. We need to get started. I'll go get Katy's gear while you round up your girls."

They left the house a half hour later in a four-wheel-drive Blazer that had been in the garage. The

SUV was white with red-and-black Flying Ace logos on the doors, the same as the pickup parked next to the driveway. All of them wouldn't have fitted in the pickup, as it had no back seat.

Laurie found it interesting, amusing and endearing that Trey seemed to experience so much angst at having to leave his daughter strapped in her car seat in the back between Carrie and Amy. He looked so guilt ridden, so heartbroken, that she very nearly volunteered to drive so he could sit in the back with his daughter.

But he was a strong man, she decided with a hidden smile. After checking for the third time to make sure Katy was strapped in securely—he even double-checked Carrie's and Amy's seat belts—he finally managed to close the backdoor and climb into the driver's seat.

Laurie saw Amy reaching a hand toward Katy. "Remember the baby rules," Laurie cautioned.

"It's okay, Mama," Amy said. "Her eyes are open, so she's awake."

"Tell me the rules so I'll know you remember all of them," Laurie said.

"Never touch her if she's asleep," Carrie said.

"You can touch her if she's awake," Amy said. "But you have to be bery careful and bery gentle, don't pull on her, and never, never, never touch her eyes."

"And never roll her onto her tummy, and never pick her up," Carrie added, "unless the house is on fire."

In the driver's seat, with his hands on the wheel,

Trey pursed his lips to keep from grinning. They were good, sound rules, and he deeply appreciated that he wouldn't have to worry about how the girls behaved around Katy. But that last bit, about unless the house was on fire, had caught him off guard and amused him, primarily because Carrie had been so serious about it.

Amusing or not, it was a damn good rule.

He realized Laurie was looking at him expectantly.

"Anything you want to add?" she asked him.

"Uh, no." He cleared his throat and put the truck in reverse. "I think you've pretty much covered it."

They were silent while he backed down the driveway and for the first couple of miles.

"When we get back," he told Laurie, "I'll leave you the keys to this vehicle in case you need to go to town or to headquarters to see Donna. After they get through with the chicken pox over there."

"I don't mind driving my own car," she offered.

"These gravel roads out here will beat your car to death in no time. Besides, this thing is sturdier. Safer."

He said it in such a way that left no room for argument. He would leave her the keys and expected her to drive the Blazer. So there.

Laurie arched a brow, but said nothing. She didn't care for dictatorial men. But he was merely looking out for her safety and that of the children, and keeping her car from possible damage. Deciding she would be a fool to argue over such an offer, she settled back to enjoy the ride.

Having seen nothing but wide-open country on her

way to the ranch, Laurie wasn't surprised to see more of the same on the way to town. Assuming she would have to make this trip on her own in the future, she paid careful attention to the turns Trey made and noted the landmarks he pointed out.

"Your first turn," he told her, "is at that big ol' split cottonwood there."

The tree was easy enough to spot. It was large—obviously old—and looked as though a bolt of lightning or God's own ax had cleaved the trunk down the middle. Half of the trunk continued to grow more or less upright, while the other half angled low and parallel with the ground. Also, it was the only thing taller than a fence post for at least a mile in any direction. Hard to miss.

They drove for fifteen miles on gravel roads before hitting two-lane blacktop for the last forty-five miles north to Hope Springs, the county seat—indeed, the only town—in Wyatt County. All three girls in the back seat fell asleep and didn't make a peep for the entire trip.

At the edge of town, the city limit sign declared a population of 2,200.

Trey pointed out the street to turn on if she needed the hospital. He drove past and pointed out the police department, sheriff's office, the schools, the video rental store, but no movie theater. There was a drugstore, Smiley's Burger Barn, the Elks Lodge and Curley's Auto Garage.

"There's Biddle's," he told her, nodding toward the grocery store. "We'll eat first, then come back."

"A wise decision," she told him. "It saves money."

"So I'm told. But at least when I shop hungry, I get home with good things to eat. Usually if I've just eaten, nothing in the store looks good, so I get home with cleaning supplies and toilet paper and not much else."

Laurie chuckled. "There is that."

Three blocks down Main Street Trey parked in front of Harvey's Café, next door to the dry cleaners. They woke the girls, and after gathering all of the paraphernalia that went along with a baby, they went inside to eat.

In Laurie's opinion Trey handled Katy and her carrier like a pro. She was beginning to wonder why he'd bothered to hire her. It didn't look to her as if he needed help with his daughter. Or wanted any help, for that matter. Laurie had yet to so much as touch the baby.

But then, he couldn't be with the baby every hour of the day. The man had a ranch to run. Or whatever it was that he did. Crops, she thought she remembered Donna saying. Trey was the farmer of the family.

That might explain the fields around his house, and why he lived there rather than at the ranch headquarters with the rest of the family.

They placed their orders, and while they waited for the food to arrive, a dozen or more people stopped by their table to say hello to Trey, make a fuss over Katy and eye Laurie and her daughters quizzically. Trey introduced them to everyone. So many names, from waitresses to deputies to store clerks to the county judge, that the names all ran together in Laurie's head.

When their food arrived Laurie's eyes bulged. The chicken-fried steak the waitress set down in front of Trey was so huge that the edges of it hung off the sides of the plate.

She made a mental note as she watched him pack it away in no time to be sure to serve him plenty of food. At least double what, in her experience, a normal man would eat.

He must work like a mule, she thought, because as near as she could tell, there wasn't an ounce of fat on that long, lean body.

When they finished eating, they loaded up and drove back to the grocery store.

There she got another eye-opener when Trey, with Katy again strapped to his chest in the baby carrier, took Laurie first to the service counter at the front of the store and introduced her to the owner, a gray-haired woman named Harriet Biddle.

"Harriet, Laurie's going to be staying out at my place taking care of Katy for a few weeks. Give her access to my account, will you?"

"Sure thing, Trey." Mrs. Biddle thumbed through a file of worn index cards and pulled one out, then stuffed it back in. "Nope, that's Jack's. Here we go." She put a card down on the counter in front of Laurie and laid a pen beside it. "Just sign your name there underneath Trey's, and you're all set. This way, anytime you come into the store, you just sign your ticket, and we'll charge it to Trey. Can't beat a deal like that, can you?"

Laurie blinked to hide her shock. A charge account in a grocery store? Just sign her name? "No," she said slowly. "I guess you can't." She looked up at Trey. "Are you sure you want to do this? I mean—"

"There's not much you can buy here but groceries. It's not like I'm giving you the key to my bank account," Trey said with a half smile. "Just sign the card and make both our lives easier. I won't always have the cash on hand to give you, and there's no need for you to spend your money and have to wait to be reimbursed."

It made such perfect sense—on the surface, at least—that Laurie found no reasonable argument. Except the one in her head that told her this just wasn't done. Regardless of Donna being her aunt, how could Trey trust her this way after knowing her for less than a day?

Still, she most certainly did not want to have to write a check on her own account to pay for his groceries, even if three of the four mouths being fed— five, counting Katy—were hers and her daughters'. The job included room and board.

With a sigh she picked up the pen and signed her name. She tried to imagine walking into her neighborhood Albertson's and asking to set up a charge account. The effort nearly made her laugh out loud.

Life in a small town was certainly different from life in the big city.

To give credit to her new employer, he didn't bat an eye when it took three shopping carts to hold all their groceries. She tried to rein in the girls when they spotted favorite treats, but they found a sneaky ally in Trey. Before she could say no, he would grab up the box or the bag and swear how much he loved that particular product and they surely couldn't do without it.

After the third different bag of cookies appeared in the shopping cart, Laurie frowned at him. "Does this job come with dental coverage?"

"Toothpaste," he said. "Let's not forget plenty of toothpaste."

Carrie and Amy both giggled.

"You've created a couple of little monsters," Laurie complained. But she was secretly pleased to see the attention he paid to the girls and how well they related to him. Lord knew their own father never paid them any attention, even before he left them.

"Am I being that bad?" Trey asked.

"What? Oh. No."

"You were sure frowning there for a minute."

"Sorry. My mind wandered." Then she frowned again, playfully this time. "But no more treats. We have more than enough. Especially by the time I add the ice cream," she muttered.

"I heard that," he said.

"Yippee!" Amy jumped up and down. "Ice cream."

Two hours later they were back at Trey's house putting the last of the groceries away. The girls were in their room, and Katy was asleep in her crib.

"This would be a good time for you to tell me how you want things done," Laurie told Trey as she folded the last of the paper sacks.

With the baby monitor beside him so he could hear Katy if she woke, Trey leaned against the counter and folded his arms across his chest. "Like Donna told you, I need you to do the cooking, the cleaning, the laundry and look after Katy."

Laurie nodded. "I understand that much. It's the details I need. What time will you expect your meals?"

"I guess I'll want breakfast at six." There were, Trey thought, more benefits to having a live-in house-keeper than he'd realized. He was used to being at Ace's by five-thirty for breakfast. Counting the driving time and feeding Katy and getting her ready, it looked as though he'd be getting at least an extra hour's sleep every night.

"Will you come home for lunch? Where do you do your work, by the way?"

"Mostly I work around here. The barn, the tractor shed, the fields. Unless they need an extra hand with the cattle or something. So, yeah, I'll be here for lunch. About noon. Six is a good time for supper."

"All right. Is there anything you don't want to eat?"

"Crepes," he managed with a straight face.

"You're in luck. I don't know how to make them."

"Good." He smiled. "I'll eat just about anything you want to fix—the plainer, the better."

"Meat and potatoes?"

"You got it."

Laurie added the paper bag to the pile of them in the corner of the pantry. "When you're home, in the house, do you want to take over any of Katy's care, or will you leave her to me?''

He gave one rueful shake of his head. "I imagine after being away from her all day I'm going to want to get my hands on her as soon as I've cleaned up. I'm kinda used to having her to myself every evening. And I imagine you're going to be wanting a break from her by then, anyway.''

Laurie smiled. "I don't know. It's been a while since I've taken care of a baby, and I miss it. But I guess I can let you hold her now and then.''

"Considering I'm her daddy, and all.''

"Considering you're her daddy.''

With every passing minute Trey felt more comfortable around Laurie Oliver—as long as he didn't look in her big green eyes for too long. Because when he did, a funny wanting feeling stirred deep down inside that he'd never felt before and didn't have a name for. It made him uneasy. So when he looked her in the eye, he made it a point not to linger.

"Come on," he told her. "While it's still light outside, I'll show you and the girls around. It's not kid-proof out there. If they're going to play outdoors, they need to know a few rules.''

Laurie frowned. "Is it dangerous?''

"There are no land mines, if that's what you mean.''

She rolled her eyes. "That's good to know. It's just that they've lived in an apartment all their lives. Their exposure to the outdoors has been in parks and in the fenced backyards of relatives, where they're never really on their own.''

"Then I'd say it's time to round out their education," Trey said. "Unless they do something outrageous, the worst they'll get out here is a skinned knee now and then."

Looking somehow doubtful and eager at the same time, Laurie finally nodded. "I'll go get the girls."

"I'll get Katy."

Watching the Oliver girls explore his world gave Trey a kick. No matter how much alike they looked, they were as different in behavior and temperament as night and day.

Carrie preferred to hold back and watch, reserve judgment. Trey could practically see her filing away in her mind every impression that came to her.

Amy, on the other hand, was full steam ahead. She ran at life full tilt, eager to see, to touch, to try everything at once.

Which, he wondered with a tightening in his throat, would Katy become? Cautious or lively?

"Oh! Look! Kitties!" The sudden excitement in Carrie's voice belied everything Trey had been thinking. The girl just hadn't been exposed to the proper stimulus until now.

Both girls squealed with delight and dropped to their knees just inside the barn door.

"They're about half-wild," Trey cautioned. "I doubt they'll let you pet them. And if they do, those baby rules of yours might come in handy."

"So we won't hurt them and they won't scratch us?"

Trey couldn't help but smile at little Amy's earnest face. "That's right."

He halfway expected Laurie to issue some warning or caution about staying away from the cats. He could see it on her face. But to her credit, all she said was, "You girls be careful around the cats, and don't chase them. Instead of catching them you'll only manage to scare them. You don't want to scare the kitties, do you?"

"Oh, no, Mama," Carrie offered. "We won't chase them. Right, Amy?"

"That's right. We won't chase the kitties."

Then Trey had to tell them that, while it was all right to go into the barn to see the cats, they were to stay out of the sheds and other outbuildings unless he or their mother was with them, because there was equipment in there that could hurt them. And they weren't to go across the road, because that was the neighbor's property, and there was a mean ol' bull over there that would just love to trample little girls.

"Wonderful," Laurie muttered. Just what had she gotten herself and her daughters into? Scratching cats, dangerous equipment and mean bulls?

Well, if she looked on the bright side, her daughters were not likely to be kidnapped right out of their yard, or hit by a car by some drunk veering up over the curb and plowing into them. That had almost happened to her parents' next-door neighbor last month.

No, all in all, rural Wyoming would be fine for them. This short stay would give the girls a chance to stretch their legs and play in the sun.

She couldn't wait for tomorrow, for her new job to begin for real.

Chapter Four

During the next few days, Trey and Laurie and the girls established a routine that seemed to be working for all of them. Gradually they were getting used to each other.

Trey had known the minute Katy entered his world that his life would never be the same. Day by day he was learning just how true that was. But Laurie and her daughters made the adjustment from bachelor household to a houseful of females if not a breeze, then easier than it could have been.

He took it in stride that first morning when he walked into the kitchen to find an attractive woman cooking his breakfast.

In stride, hell. He thought he'd died and gone to heaven. The smell of coffee that had lured him from bed hadn't hurt anything, either.

Carrie and Amy had still been asleep, which was expected. Not even the sun was up at that hour.

"Smells good," he told Laurie. "How's Katy?"

"Still sleeping."

They'd argued the night before about who would take the baby monitor to bed. Trey was used to doing it. Katy was *his* daughter, after all. He didn't plan to give up *all* responsibility for her, only her daytime care while he was working.

"Besides," he'd told Laurie. "I'm blessed, or so they tell me. She usually sleeps through the night."

"Then it won't matter if I take the monitor, will it? It's what you're paying me to do."

She'd worn a look of pure stubbornness on her face. Trey had given in, but it hadn't been much of a concession, really. If Katy had cried, he was certain he would have heard her, monitor or not. Her room was right next to his.

Still, it wouldn't hurt to ask. "Did she wake you up during the night?"

"She never made a peep, the little darling. I changed and fed her when I got up, then she went right back to sleep."

It felt odd knowing someone else had been up and tending to his baby and he hadn't known it. Hadn't heard a thing. "You've been up awhile, then."

"About an hour. How do you want your eggs?"

And so it began, the new routine.

He came in for lunch at noon, and it was a pure pleasure to get to hold Katy after he washed up and to have someone else prepare his meal. And sharing that meal with Laurie and her daughters had been no hardship, either. If he wasn't careful, those two young Oliver ladies were going to steal his heart. And if he wasn't more careful, their mother was going to stir things in him he had no place feeling for the hired help.

That night when he came in to supper, he stepped through the backdoor into the kitchen and something odd happened. It wasn't as if he hadn't known Laurie and the girls would be there. Of course he had. He'd hired her, hadn't he? Seen her at breakfast and lunch.

But something about walking through the door at the end of the day and finding a roomful of females laughing and talking and carrying food to the table hit him somewhere deep inside. The only word he could think of to describe what he felt was *yearning*.

Was this what had been missing from his life? This feeling of family?

But aside from Katy, lying on her back waving her arms in the air in her playpen in the corner, this wasn't his family.

"There you are." Laurie smiled warmly at him. "Supper will be ready in fifteen minutes, so you've got time to clean up if you want."

He looked down at the dirt covering his jeans. "You think I need it?"

"Not on my account," she answered. "The only thing I care about is that your face and hands are clean. The rest of you is fine as far as I'm concerned."

"With an attitude like that, I can't believe some man hasn't grabbed you up."

Glancing around to find the girls sitting on the floor

beside the playpen, Laurie looked back at Trey. "Some man did. It didn't take him long before he decided to ungrab me."

"She means we're divorced," Amy piped up cheerfully. "Our home is broken."

"Amy." Laurie whirled toward her daughter. "Where on earth did you hear a thing like that?"

Amy shrugged, unconcerned. "From you."

"I've never said we have a broken home, because we don't."

"*You* said we were divorced. Grandma said we were poor little lambs and came from a broken home."

"Excuse me a minute," Laurie said to Trey, a muscle tensing along her jaw. "I need to clear this up."

Unless Trey missed his guess, that was murder he read in her eyes before she blanked it out, and it was directed at Grandma.

The decent thing for him to do in that moment would be to make himself scarce and give Laurie the privacy to talk to her daughters. But he knew he might never have another opportunity to learn about little girls and how to deal with them once he found a permanent housekeeper and Laurie and her girls went home. He was staying, and he was taking notes.

But he could at least act as if he wasn't eavesdropping. He went to the sink and started washing his hands.

Laurie crossed to her daughters and knelt down between them. She smoothed a hand over Amy's golden hair. "Honey, Daddy didn't divorce you and Carrie."

"He just divorced you?" Amy asked, her eyes big.

"Or did you divorce him?" Leave it to Carrie to ask that one.

Laurie placed her other arm around Carrie's shoulders. "It's like I told you before, he and I divorced each other."

Carrie nodded. "Because you were both happier apart."

At the sink Trey was afraid to turn off the water, afraid the sudden quiet would remind them he was standing there. God, how did Laurie do it, raise those girls on her own, answer questions that must tear her apart.

What kind of man would leave a family like this to fend for themselves?

A lowlife, that's who, Trey thought with sudden anger on Laurie and her girls' behalf.

"And Grandma was wrong about our house," Laurie told them. "Broken home is an expression some people use when there's a divorce in the family. But it's not a very nice thing to say."

"When something's broken," Carrie said, her small face lined in concentration, "you have to fix it, or you have to throw it away, because it's no good anymore."

"That's right. And we're not broken, are we?" Laurie hugged both girls to her sides. "Nothing about us needs fixing. We're doing just fine, don't you think?" She finished by slipping a hand down to each girl's ribs and tickling them, making them break out in giggles.

Trey's admiration for Laurie Oliver rose about a hundred notches.

"My hat is off to you, lady," he murmured to her a moment later when she joined him at the sink. "You were brilliant."

"I was sick to my stomach," she confessed. "Just wait until I get my hands on my mother. Broken home, indeed," she added with a hiss. "Is *matricide* a word?"

"I think it is."

That night after the girls and Katy were in bed Trey had another new experience. Sharing the sudden quiet with someone.

While he sat in his recliner, Laurie lowered herself to the sofa with a sigh. "You hear that?"

"I don't hear anything," he said.

She smiled and closed her eyes. "Yeah. First time all day. Nice, isn't it?"

Trey chuckled. "What, one day on the job and you're already done in?"

"Not done in." With her eyes still closed, her smile widened. "Just pleasantly tired."

Trey watched her for a long moment as she leaned back on the sofa and propped her feet on the ottoman. He couldn't recall ever having shared such a peaceful moment with another woman. Outside of bed, at least.

Something about this woman tugged at him. He began to understand that she stirred up that long-buried yearning in him for a woman of his own. A family of his own.

On a long breath, he leaned his head back and raised the footrest on his chair. Might as well get that idea right out of his head where this woman was concerned. She was temporary. She had plans, a life to return to in a few weeks.

Beside the fact that she was damn good-looking and he felt a strong, heathy attraction to her, he figured his biggest problem was proximity. She was here, in his home, sharing his daily life.

That, and the fact that he hadn't been with a woman in months.

Yeah, right, pal. Who was he kidding? He could have had his way with an entire harem for the past month and Laurie Oliver would still attract him.

But he knew better than to hit on her. She was his employee. She trusted him to treat her with respect. And that meant hands off, bub.

So, hands off it would be.

But he wished, desperately, that when he looked at her again, he hadn't caught her staring at him with a look of curiosity in her eyes.

She looked away instantly, but a telltale blush stained her cheeks.

Laurie couldn't sleep that night. She lay awake and scolded herself for getting caught staring at Trey like some teenager going ga-ga over a rock star.

Trey Wilder was no rock star. He was a down-to-earth—literally, she thought with a snicker—farmer. It was just that he was so pleasurable to look at, with those cobalt blue eyes and that raven-black hair.

And that voice. She had yet to get used to the way the muscles in her shoulders and the backs of her legs went slack whenever he spoke, while other, more private muscles tensed.

Get a grip, girl.

He was her boss, for heaven's sake. He was part of the family that employed her aunt. And Laurie was here only for a few weeks, to look after his daughter and his house, because he'd been careless enough to get some girl pregnant, and the girl wanted nothing to do with him or the baby.

Whoever she was, the woman must have been out of her mind to come to a decision like that.

Then again, Jimmy was a handsome devil and charming when he wanted to be. He had certainly charmed her. The only good things to come of that were Carrie and Amy. Laurie wouldn't trade her daughters for the world, so she couldn't regret having fallen for Jimmy.

So maybe Katy's mother had her reasons for not wanting anything to do with Trey. After all, what did Laurie really know about him other than what Donna told her? Besides, Donna loved him like a son, so she wasn't exactly objective.

But, according to Donna, Katy's mother tried to give the baby up for adoption without even letting Trey know he was a father.

That, in Laurie's book, was wrong, any way she looked at it. There was no excuse to deny a man that knowledge.

Laurie was just glad, for Trey's and Katy's sakes, that the woman's plans had fallen through. It was more than obvious that Trey and Katy belonged together.

*   *   *

Laurie spent the next couple of days giving the house a thorough cleaning, front to back, top to bottom. She washed and ironed curtains, vacuumed beneath and behind furniture and declared war on the soap scum, hard-water deposits and mildew in Trey's shower.

If from time to time she found herself looking out a window with the hope of catching a glimpse of her employer, well, no one but her knew it. And after all, she wasn't dead, was she? She could appreciate the sight of a tall, lean man in snug-fitting jeans.

This afternoon, however, she couldn't see him at all. He had driven off across the ranch in his pickup after lunch, muttering something about irrigation. She thought maybe he meant to work on the watering system for his crops, but, city girl that she was, that was only a guess.

In the backyard, Carrie and Amy were playing with their dolls in the shade of a big elm. They had taken to outdoor play like a couple of ducks to a pond. If nothing else, Laurie would always be grateful for this chance her daughters had to experience the outdoors without so many of the worries and problems prevalent in a big city.

With Katy in her arms, Laurie turned away from the kitchen window and placed the empty nurser on the counter. "How about it, young lady? Are you ready to give me another big burp?" After placing a cloth over her shoulder, she positioned the baby and gently rubbed and patted her back.

From outside came the crunching sound of tires on gravel.

"Donna." Laurie rushed out the door to greet her

aunt. They had spoken on the phone a couple of times but had yet to see each other since Laurie's arrival.

"I couldn't stand it another minute," Donna declared. "I escaped the chicken pox so I could get over here and see you."

"Aunt Donna!" Carrie and Amy barreled around the corner of the house and into Donna's widespread arms.

"Oh, my, how you girls have grown since Christmas."

"Come on inside," Laurie invited. "I just made a fresh pitcher of iced tea."

"You sold me, but I can't stay long. I left Belinda manning the fort alone."

They gathered around the kitchen table with glasses of iced tea and a plate of cookies.

"How are you three getting along here?" Donna asked. "Is Trey giving you any trouble?"

"Mr. Trey is cool," Amy announced. "He's got kitties in his barn, but they won't let us pet them 'cause they're mostly wild."

"Well, now." Donna looked suitably impressed. "In a few days you'll have to come over to headquarters for a visit. The boys can show you around. They've got some barn cats, too, and they have a dog, and horses and cows."

The ever-practical Carrie's eyes widened. She'd been drawing pictures of horses for the past six months in hopes of convincing her mother to buy her one. "Can we go there, Mama? Can we?"

"When the boys are over their chicken pox, and when it's convenient for Aunt Donna and Mrs. Wilder. Now, you can each take one more cookie and go outside again.''

Donna stayed a few more minutes, but then had to get back to her duties. She made Laurie promise to bring the girls for a visit as soon as the boys were well.

Laurie chuckled. ''Since they've got horses, I don't think I'm going to have a choice.''

When Trey returned home shortly before supper, he was pulling a horse trailer behind his pickup. With Katy strapped to her chest, Laurie took Carrie and Amy outside to watch him unload a beautiful gray gelding into the corral beside the barn.

Coming as it did on the heels of Donna's mention of horses, Laurie knew she was going to be in for a hard time. Carrie was already beside herself, and Amy would start drooling any minute, she was so excited.

''It's a horse,'' Carrie cried, forgetting completely that she was the sober sister. ''Mr. Trey, you have a horse.''

Trey had just backed the horse out of the trailer. Holding on to the lead, he turned and saw them approaching.

The girls dashed forward.

''Not too close,'' Laurie called.

Trey's heart took a leap behind his ribs. Countless times he'd trailered a horse home, but never to the excitement of little girls. God, look at them, he thought, running to meet him, their eyes bright and shining and glued to the horse. He didn't need a crystal ball to know a love affair was in the making. Two love affairs. The girls were instantly in love with the horse, and Trey was falling hard for two little sweet-hearts.

"Hey, ladies," he said.

They giggled. They always giggled when he called them ladies.

"This is Soldier," he told them. "Don't get near his hind legs. He likes to kick, and he can kick real hard."

A little more cautious now, but no less excited, the girls moved away from the horse's hindquarters and toward Trey.

"Golly, Mr. Trey." Amy's eyes were about to pop out of her head. "Is he yours?"

"When I need him, he's mine."

Carrie gaped up at the horse, then at Trey. "Does that mean you're a cowboy?"

"Sometimes."

"Huh?" Amy scrunched up her sweet little face. "How can you be a cowboy only sometimes?"

"When I'm working cows, I'm a cowboy. When I work the fields," he said, waving toward the acres of alfalfa, "I'm more of a farmer. When we have a family meeting to take care of business, I'm a rancher."

"Golly." Clearly impressed, Amy looked at him in awe. "Are you gonna ride him?"

"Tomorrow. I have to go fix some downed fence, and I can't get there in the pickup or the Blazer, so Soldier's going to take me there."

"Will you be a cowboy then?"

Trey hooked his thumbs in his front jeans pockets

and kicked at the ground in his best "aw, shucks" imitation. "Reckon so, little lady," he drawled.

Both girls squealed with delight. Even Laurie laughed, although she came no closer.

To his credit, Soldier didn't flinch from the high-pitched squeals.

"Aunt Donna says they have horses over at the…at the…whadayacallit," Amy said. "Where she lives."

"Headquarters?"

"Yeah. That place. She said we could see their horses."

"She did, huh?"

"Uh-huh." Amy nodded her head vigorously.

Trey was puzzled. As excited as both girls obviously were, they hadn't made a move to touch the horse. That could be because the animal was so big and they were so small. But they hadn't asked to touch him. And the really odd part, to him, was that they hadn't asked if they could ride him. What kid worth his or her salt didn't want to ride a horse?

The thing was, they did want to ride Soldier, Trey was sure of it. He could see the fierce longing in their eyes. But neither of them asked.

He was hesitant to offer without talking to their mother about it first, though, so maybe he could lead them to ask.

"Do you want to pet him?" A glance at Laurie told him she wasn't averse to that idea.

Amy and Carrie each sucked in a huge breath. "Would it be all right, do you think?" Carrie looked over at her mother.

"Can we really pet him?" Amy was practically jumping up and down.

"Well." Trey dragged the word out. "I guess you can, but we have to make a deal first."

Laurie stood nearby watching with a small smile.

Okay, Trey thought. That was good. No objections from Mama.

"What kind of deal?" Carrie wanted to know.

"You can pet him when I'm with you, and you can never, ever go into the corral when any animal bigger than a kitty is in there. Do I have your word?"

"Yes, sir," they said in unison.

"Fair enough."

One by one he lifted each girl and showed her how to stroke the horse's nose and jaw, the two places he liked best.

Trey was sorely tempted to simply swing each girl up onto Soldier's bare back and lead the animal around the yard. Before Katy, he would have done it without a thought. On the Flying Ace, kids rode horses.

But these girls were not his children. He had no right to make a decision such as allowing them to ride a horse.

Not wanting to get too close while she had the baby with her, Laurie watched from a few yards away. Her daughters were in heaven. Trey could have no idea how much this meant to them.

Nor, she thought with a silent, good-natured groan, could he have any idea of the time she was going to be in for, now that they'd been up close and personal with a real, live horse.

To forestall the inevitable questions about getting a horse of their own, as soon as each girl had petted the horse, Laurie called them to go inside and wash up so they could help her set the table.

She turned to follow them, but Trey called to her.

"Laurie, hold up a minute." He tied the horse's lead to a rail on the corral fence, then crossed the dusty ground to her side.

"What is it?" she asked.

"Why didn't they ask if they could ride him?"

Laurie frowned. "What do you mean?"

"The girls. It was all over their faces how bad they wanted to ride, but they didn't ask."

"You didn't offer."

"I didn't know if you'd already told them they weren't allowed to. So what's the deal?"

Laurie glanced down at Katy, the better to hide should her emotions show in her face as her heart sank. She hadn't realized it herself, perhaps because she hadn't wanted to, but Trey was right. Both girls had been dying to get up on the horse's back.

Oh, they'd been doing so much better lately, despite the tension in their grandparents' house. Looking back on those weeks at her parents', Laurie realized that the constant little battles with their uncle Billy over volume control had helped make the girls a little more assertive. Carrie in particular.

Yet Laurie recalled that, even then, Carrie had never asked her grandfather for anything.

It was the rule. The girls had made a rule that they thought she didn't know about. It stipulated that if you had to ask a man for it—whatever *it* was—and it was important to you, the answer was going to be no. Or if it was yes, the promised toy or television show or outing would never come to be. If you asked a man for anything, you were probably going to be disappointed.

Thanks, Jimmy, you jerk.

But Laurie bore plenty of blame on her own. She should have filed for divorce years ago, when she first realized Jimmy was never going to grow up. That had been shortly after Amy's birth.

If only. If Laurie had divorced Jimmy then, her babies would have grown-up happier. She would have seen to it.

Oh, God, her heart would be in her throat the entire time they were on horseback. But that was her problem, not theirs. She wanted them to ride a horse, because they wanted it so desperately.

"Laurie?" Trey prodded.

"No." She looked up and met his gaze. "No, I've never told them they're not allowed. You're right, I know they would love it. But I've never ridden, so I don't know what to do."

"As long as you're okay with it, I'll handle it. I'll just lead them around in the corral for a few minutes."

Laurie let out a breath. "Thank you, Trey. This is going to mean the world to them."

"How about we do it after supper? We'll still have plenty of light."

Laurie swallowed. Maybe somewhere in the back of her mind she'd thought she would have a day or two to get used to the idea of her babies riding a horse. But it was better this way. Less time to fret. Even if it did mean they would be so excited afterward that she'd probably never get them to sleep tonight.

"We could do it now if you'd rather," Trey offered.

"Oh." She thought a moment, then took a deep breath and nodded. "Yes. If you don't mind, let's do it now. I'll go get them."

And what, Trey wondered as she turned away and went into the house, was that all about?

He might never know what had been going through Laurie's mind while she'd thought about her girls riding horseback. But he knew how the girls felt about the results of all that heavy thinking. He could hear their shrieks of delight clear out in the yard.

Chapter Five

To make it official, and to give the girls something to hold on to besides Soldier's mane, which would be hard to reach for their short arms, Trey saddled the horse.

Of course, it was his saddle, so it was nearly as big as an armchair, but they loved it.

First he put them up together and led the horse around the corral. Pretty tame stuff, but the girls loved it.

He kept one eye on them and their mount, and the other on their mother. She was handling herself, Laurie was. She was as nervous as a hen with one chick, but she was smiling.

Even Katy seemed to enjoy the show, although Trey didn't figure she could see it well enough to make out anything.

Suddenly Laurie sucked in a sharp breath. "The camera. Oh. Trey, don't let them get down. I have to get the camera."

Cradling Katy in her arms, she rushed toward the house. When she came back out a few minutes later she had a camera slung around her neck and was wheeling Katy in the carriage.

By the time Laurie got Katy's carriage situated and was ready to take pictures, Carrie and Amy were feeling confident enough up there on Soldier's back to mug for the camera.

After a while Trey had them each ride alone for several minutes. When Laurie told them they'd done enough riding for one day, they reluctantly prepared to go back inside.

But Trey wasn't finished. He took the camera from her and handed it to Carrie. "Do you know how to work this?"

"Sure."

"Good."

"What am I supposed to take pictures of?"

Trey winked. "You'll figure it out."

Then he turned, grabbed Laurie around the waist and swung her up into the saddle.

Laurie shrieked, then grabbed on to the saddle horn with both hands, as she'd seen her daughters do.

"Trey, what are you doing?"

"Giving Mama a ride."

"Smile, Mama," Carrie called.

Laurie smiled.

Carrie snapped a picture, then another.

Laurie glanced down at Trey, her smile taking on a feral appearance. "I'll get you for this, Mr. Trey."

Trey grinned. "Promises, promises. Come on, Soldier, let's give the lady a ride." With a small tug on the reins from Trey, the horse started walking.

At the sudden movement beneath her, Laurie shrieked in earnest and hung on for dear life.

At the corral fence, Carrie and Amy cheered. Amy clapped while Carrie took pictures.

"Okay," Laurie called down from what seemed like her mile-high perch. "This is plenty, Trey. We can stop now."

"Stop?" He halted the animal.

Thank God, Laurie thought. At least she hadn't fallen off and made a fool of herself in front of her girls. And Trey.

Just when she thought he was going to help her down, he instead swung up behind her.

"Trey," she cried. Now not only did she have to worry about falling on her head—or her butt—she had to worry about melting into a pool right there in the saddle. She was surrounded by him. His arms curved around hers, his chest pressed flush against her back. His warmth—*heat*—enveloped her.

Then he removed his left hand from the reins and placed it, fingers splayed, across her abdomen. "What are you doing?" she managed.

"Taking you for a ride."

No kidding.

"Amy," he called, "can you open the gate?"

"Oh, Trey, no, that's not necessary. You don't have to—"

Amy opened the gate.

"Hold on," Trey said.

"To what?" Laurie cried.

"To the saddle horn. Or my arms. Or my legs. Whatever you can reach."

Well, now. Just how was she supposed to take that comment?

"Girls, keep an eye on Katy. We'll keep it nice and slow," he added to Laurie.

Oh, she thought. *Oh.* He was seducing her without even trying. His lips were next to her ear, and his voice sent shivers down her spine that had nothing to do with her fear of falling off a horse.

He took the horse at a slow walk around the house.

The advantages of riding double were many. Trey was so taken with the sweet smell of Laurie's hair, and the sweeter feel of her in his arms, that the slow walk around the house seemed to last only seconds. When they returned to the corral he was loath to dismount. He wanted to turn the horse away and take off across the fields, ride over the far ridge down to the creek.

There he would dismount amid the willows and soft summer grass, beside the water trickling down from the mountains. He would lay her down on the grass and—

"Was it fun, Mama?"

Trey reluctantly pulled himself back from the brink of bliss and drew the horse to a halt in the center of the corral.

It was Amy, still bouncing with excitement, who had spoken, but Laurie had not answered.

Trey dipped his head until his lips brushed her ear. "Was it, Mama?"

She turned her head slightly toward him and, with narrowed eyes, asked, "Are you doing that on purpose?"

Trey blinked and grinned. "Doing what?"

The girls were so wound up about getting to ride a horse that it was all they could do to stay in their seats long enough to eat supper. Afterward, a family sitcom on television finally held their attention, but Laurie had little hope that she would be able to get them to sleep at their regular time that night.

When she finished cleaning up the kitchen after supper, she smoothed lotion on her hands and made her way to the living room, where the girls were sprawled on the floor. Trey was in his recliner, chuckling along with them, Katy held securely and lovingly in his arms.

Laurie took a seat on the sofa and waited until the program ended. "Anybody want ice cream?"

"Yeah!" Amy and Carrie scrambled up.

"Sounds good to me." Trey narrowed his eyes and smiled. "Are you serving?"

"I'm serving the children, in the kitchen. If you want any you'll have to come with us."

He laughed. "I was afraid you'd say that. Okay, sweet pea, let's get up and put you in your playpen while your old man makes a pig of himself."

Laurie dished up a bowl of chocolate for each of the girls, then took pity on Trey and got his, too, then served herself.

"You're a gem," Trey told her.

"I'll bet you say that to all your housekeepers."

"Since you're the only one I've ever had, I guess you're right. Speaking of which, did anyone call about the ad today?"

She shook her head. "No. I'm sorry. Where is it running?"

"I started out in the *Wyatt County Gazette,* but now it's running in Rock Springs, Pinedale and Jackson Hole. If I don't get any results soon, I guess I'll try Cheyenne, although I doubt anyone would want to move this far."

"They would if they could see it," Laurie said.

"Really?"

"It's heaven out here," she said. "All that wide-open space, the mountains in the background. Fresh air. Quiet."

"You like it here, then?"

"What's not to like? It's wonderful. And the girls love it, don't you, girls?"

"Yeah, it's cool," Amy said. "Kitties and horses and a yard and everything."

Trey smiled. He was glad they liked it here. It made him feel good to know Laurie and her daughters enjoyed the land he loved. "Maybe I'll let you guys write the next ad. One woman called the week before you came. She sounded perfect for the job, but when she realized how isolated we are out here she couldn't hang up fast enough."

"Her loss," Laurie told him.

Not mine, he thought. If he'd hired that woman, he might never have met this woman who, with her laughter and her daughters, had somehow turned his house into a home.

"I'm through." Carrie let her spoon clink against the bowl.

"Me, too," said Amy. "Can we watch more TV now?"

"For a little while. Carry your bowls to the counter."

Carefully, using both hands, each girl carried her bowl to the counter and placed it next to the sink.

Carrie snuggled up against her mother and put an arm around her neck. "Thank you for the ice cream, Mama." She kissed Laurie on the cheek.

"Me, too." Amy angled in and placed a kiss on Laurie's other cheek.

"You're welcome, both of you." Before she turned them loose, Laurie kissed the tip of each little nose.

Watching the girls' open affection for their mother had Trey wondering, hoping Katy would love him that much. Would she mind not having a mother? Or would he meet a woman someday who would become her mother?

It was too much to think about. Too far in the future. For now he was simply grateful to be allowed to watch the interaction between a mother and her daughters.

He finished his ice cream, then waited for Laurie to finish hers before he took her bowl and his to the sink. There he rinsed them all and stacked them, as she already had the dishwasher running.

When he turned from the sink, she was there. Close. He didn't think; he placed one hand on the side of her neck and kissed her cheek. "Thanks for the ice cream."

Laurie couldn't move. She hadn't seen that maneuver coming. How could she have? One minute they were talking about his ad and eating ice cream, and the next he was imitating her girls and giving her a thank-you kiss.

But he should have backed away then. Laughed at the silly joke. But he didn't. She stared up at him, mesmerized, unable to think straight and watched the laughter in his bright-blue eyes turn to heat.

Oh, God, he was going to kiss her again. For real this time. What was she going to do? How had they ended up alone together? She wanted to run. She wanted to hide.

She wanted…to kiss him.

Trey could feel her breath puffing soft and warm against his chin. Beneath his hand he felt her tremble. "Laurie?"

She swallowed hard. "What?"

He gazed down into her eyes and wanted to fall in and never come out. "I want to kiss you." He was stunned at just how badly he wanted it.

"You just did," she whispered.

With the tip of his nose, he nuzzled her cheek. It was silky soft. "Not the way I want to."

Laurie felt her knees threaten to buckle. His voice had always gotten to her, but when he whispered low and soft against her skin this way, she had no defense at all.

But she would try. She had to try, didn't she? Although why escaped her at that moment. Still… "We shouldn't," she managed.

"You're right. We shouldn't." He smoothed his lips along her cheekbone. "But I still want to." He trailed his mouth down to her jaw. "So do you."

She did. Heaven help her, she wanted his mouth on hers, his hands on her body. Anywhere. Everywhere. The strength of the wanting shocked her. "Trey."

"Say yes, Laurie," he whispered.

With a low moan she did.

Cupping her face in both hands, Trey moved that final fraction of an inch and kissed her.

Her mouth was cool from the ice cream, and sweet from her. Her taste was dark and rich. The hands that grasped his wrists were delicate yet strong. He nipped and tasted and dove in for more.

Laurie let him pull her closer, until their bodies were flush against each other. His was all firm, hard muscle—and warm…so warm. His touch on her face was gentle, in sharp contrast with the suddenly ravenous way he took her mouth. He quite simply overwhelmed her senses. From his hot, secret taste to the clean smell of soap on his skin to the firmness of his body. She savored all of him and let her mind go blank.

Trey felt the subtle changes in her, the speeding of her pulse, the softening of her body. She was both generous and demanding, yielding yet not submissive in the least. And he wanted more. He wanted all she would give him.

But not here, not now, with three little girls in the

next room, two of them old enough to ask questions neither he nor, he suspected, Laurie, were prepared to answer.

So he ended the kiss, amazed at how hard it was to make himself release her lips. Amazed further at how hard it was to catch his breath.

Laurie's eyelids had never felt so heavy when she raised them. It was her daughters' laughter from the living room that jolted her back, and away from Trey. "I, uh, better go give the girls their baths." She turned to leave.

"Laurie?"

Breathless from the kiss, from the fear that she should never, ever, have gotten that close to this man, she stopped.

His voice, when it came, slid all over her like warm honey. "We're going to want to do that again. Soon."

She shook her head. "I don't think that's a good idea. You're my boss. I work for you. It's not right."

"Well, then." He rocked back on his heels and pushed his hands into the front pockets of his jeans. "I guess I'll just have to give you a day off, won't I?"

What had he meant, give her a day off?

Laurie hadn't stayed around to find out, hadn't had the nerve to ask. Because the look in his eyes seemed to say that if she had a day off, when he wasn't her boss and she wasn't his employee, then all bets would be off.

"Oh, Laurie," she whispered to herself in the darkness of her room late that night. "What have you done?"

Nothing, she assured herself. Nothing terrible, anyway. It was just a kiss. She would simply put it out of her mind. Just because it was a kiss like none she'd ever had before didn't mean she had to let it mean anything.

It probably meant less than nothing to Trey. A man with his looks, his charm, probably had women lined up to kiss him.

That thought followed her into a restless sleep and left her unexplainably depressed the next morning when Katy woke her at the usual time. Laurie let the joy of caring for such a good-natured baby ease away her residual feelings from the night before. Bathing the child soothed her.

"Come on, Katy-girl, give me a smile," she coaxed.

Always happy to oblige, Katy cooed and smiled and waved her tiny hands in the air.

"Oh, and aren't you clever, and isn't that the prettiest smile I've ever seen. Now that you're all clean and sweet smelling again, I bet you're hungry."

A few minutes later Laurie was seated in Trey's recliner feeding Katy her morning bottle when Trey walked into the room.

Sudden visions of their kiss sent heat flaming to Laurie's cheeks. How was she supposed to act around him the morning after a kiss like that? What was she supposed to say?

What came out of her mouth was, "You're up early."

He gave a negligent shrug and leaned down to stroke Katy's cheek. "How's my girl this morning?"

"She's fine. If you want to take over I'll start your breakfast."

Trey shrugged again. "Sure." Hell. She wouldn't look him in the eye. She'd been right last night, that kiss had not been a good idea. And not just because she was his employee and, if she were the type, she could sue him for sexual harassment. Wouldn't that be just dandy. And dammit, he would deserve it. Except...

Except she'd wanted it, too. And she'd kissed him back.

That was the other reason he shouldn't have kissed her. He'd taken the feel of her, the taste of her, with him into his sleep. Three times during the night he had wakened in a pool of sweat, his blood pumping hot and fast while his arms reached for her and found nothing but air.

But in his dreams she had filled his arms. He'd dreamed that instead of breaking off the kiss, he had taken her—they had taken each other—right there on the kitchen table. And up against the refrigerator. And the washing machine, during the spin cycle.

And if he thought about those erotic dreams now, he'd never make it through breakfast. He had to get over this sudden obsession with household appliances.

As awkward as the morning had been, Laurie wished the girls had been up to watch Trey ride off on horseback just as the sun broke free in the east.

There stood the little prairie wife, waving her cowboy off to a hard day in the saddle.

"Yeah, right." With a snort of self-directed laughter she turned away and finished loading the dishwasher.

Ordinarily Trey would have trailered Soldier as far as possible toward the break in the fence, until it wasn't safe to drive any farther, before going the rest of his way on horseback. But he wasn't in a particular hurry this morning and it wasn't all that far—just impossible to get to without risking tearing up a vehicle, even a four-wheel-drive.

But the real reason he'd decided to load his tools and supplies behind the saddle and spend the morning astride a horse was for the quiet. Riding alone across the land soothed him in a way nothing else could, except perhaps standing in the middle of a heathy stand of hay.

The hayfields, however, weren't isolated enough to suit him today. He had some thinking to do. And maybe after he'd repaired the fence and ridden home, he would talk a certain mother into letting him give her girls a ride around the corral.

The first time he'd come home for supper and found Laurie and her girls there waiting for him had rocked him. He'd had the fleeting thought that that was what it would be like to have a family of his own.

He'd gotten used to them, though, and understood that they weren't his family. But this morning, when he'd walked into his living room before sunup and found Laurie in his chair feeding his daughter...

Ah, hell. She was supposed to be just a woman, temporary help until he could hire a housekeeper, nothing more. He wasn't supposed to be drawn to her this way. He wasn't supposed to want her.

But he did want her. Was he supposed to just ignore that? Unless he'd forgotten everything he ever knew about women, she was right there with him last night every step of the way. If they had been alone, if he wasn't her employer but simply a man she felt an attraction for, last night might—would—have turned out differently. Neither of them would have slept alone.

In frustration, he tugged off his hat and ran his fingers through his hair. Hell, what was he doing obsessing about a kiss, a woman, anyway? If the tables were turned and she was the one pursuing him, he wouldn't trust her as far as he could pick her up and throw her.

Of course, that was because he'd been burned. Scorched to cinders. His heart left in ashes.

His heart wasn't involved here.

Nothing was involved. Last night he'd shared a kiss with a beautiful, sexy woman. This morning she hadn't been able to look him in the eye. He would back off, give her the room she deserved and seemed to want. If there was nothing more, then there was nothing more.

Dammit, he wanted more.

By the time Carrie and Amy got up, Laurie had cleaned the main bathroom she and the girls used, as well as the master bath off Trey's bedroom, and she had stripped all the unoccupied beds. But the girls liked to help her put on clean sheets, so she saved that chore for after they'd eaten breakfast.

Since Trey wasn't expected back for lunch, Laurie got the girls to help her make sandwiches, and they had a picnic under the elm in the backyard. They took Katy with them, of course, and spread an old blanket beneath its limbs. After they ate, Laurie read to them from one of the girls' favorite storybooks. When their heads started drooping, along with their eyelids, she shooed them back into the house for a nap.

She intended to run the vacuum, but waited until after nap time, when she sent the girls outside to play. After vacuuming the carpet, she decided she was sufficiently calm to call her mother.

"Honey, when are you coming home?" Her mother's plaintive question made it sound as if Laurie and the girls had been gone for months.

"The middle of August, Mom, as I told you before."

"I just can't stand the thought of you taking those sweet babies off to the wilds of Wyoming. Why, that place where Donna works is the back of beyond."

With a smile Laurie remembered the endless miles of sagebrush and sparse grass and not much else. "It's nice here, but that's not why I called."

"Did you get in touch with Jimmy before you left?"

Laurie rolled her eyes. It was no secret that Susan Harris adored Jimmy Oliver and thought he could do no wrong. Laurie had shed many a tear into her pillow at night over the fact that her own mother hadn't supported her during the divorce. Now, more than a year later, the hurt had changed to anger, which Laurie tried desperately to swallow.

When she had learned that her apartment complex was being leveled and that she and the girls needed a temporary place to live until their house became available, her parents had not hesitated to invite them to spend the summer with them. But before Laurie had accepted, she'd made her mother promise to lay off on the subject of Jimmy Oliver. Susan had agreed, and Laurie had thought things were fine, at least on that front. Until Amy's innocent comment about their "broken home" last night.

"Honey, did you call him?" her mother asked again.

"You know I didn't."

"That's a mistake, honey, if you don't mind my saying."

"I do mind, Mom."

"You're just making it that much harder for the two of you to get back together, taking off this way without a word to him."

"Mother." Laurie dragged the word out through gritted teeth. "I am *not* going back with Jimmy, not ever, and I'm insulted that you think I should. He's a weak, irresponsible boy who never grew up. He doesn't need a wife, he needs a mother. And if you'll recall, he's the one who decided he didn't want to be tied down anymore with a wife and two children."

Over the phone came a long-suffering sigh. "Wild

oats, honey. I told you at the time, he just needed to sow a few wild oats.''

It was the same song and dance every time Laurie made the mistake of letting her mother bring up Jimmy. Laurie was so sick of it she could scream.

"I didn't call because I wanted a lecture, Mom.''

"I'm sure you didn't, honey, but now and then it seems like you need one.''

"Well, this time I'm *giving* the lecture.''

There was a length of silence before her mother spoke again. "Oh?''

"Yes, oh. You told my daughters they had a broken home.''

"Well…''

"That they were poor little lambs who came from a broken home.''

"Well, it's true, isn't it?''

"Our home is not broken, Mom, and Carrie and Amy are not poor little lambs. The only time I ever want to hear of you calling them that is if they're sick or injured.''

"Mind your tone, Laurie. I'm still your mother.''

"And I'm their mother, and I don't want them exposed to that kind of talk. There's no need for them to learn to feel sorry for themselves or to think there's something wrong with the way we live. Since you obviously haven't been paying attention, both girls are much happier since Jimmy left, because now they don't have to live with someone who ignores them while he's in the room with them, and who stayed in the same room with them as little as possible. He hurt them, Mom, with his indifference and his immaturity.

He hurt my babies, and I don't ever want to hear you tell me I should go back with him again.''

"Well," her mother said. "I'm sorry that I've obviously upset you, honey.'' But she didn't sound sorry. "Oops, that's the doorbell. Gotta run. Kiss the girls for me.''

"Mom—'' But her mother had already hung up.

Laurie spent the next several moments trying not to beat her head against the nearest wall. Then she took two aspirin for the headache that had zoomed in during the phone call and went to check on Katy.

There was no real need to check on her. She was asleep in her crib, just as she'd been when Laurie last checked on her, right before she'd called home, and there hadn't been a peep of sound coming through the baby monitor. But Katy was such a pleasure to look at, so sweet and pretty, that it soothed the raw nerves Laurie was left with from talking with her mother.

Heavens, she was going to miss this sweet little baby when it was time to go.

Feeling much better for having watched an infant's innocent sleep, Laurie made her way back to the kitchen, where she mixed together the ingredients for a meat loaf and put it in the refrigerator to keep until later. Trey should be back soon. She would wait until she saw him coming before she started supper.

She was standing at the kitchen sink a few minutes later drying her hands on a dish towel when she heard the scream.

Chapter Six

Trey had finished repairing the fence and rode home at a leisurely pace. Nothing else was pressing today, and he'd worked out in his mind that he wasn't going to pressure Laurie into anything, so he was enjoying the ride.

Almost home now, acre after acre of green alfalfa stretched out before him. In the distance he could see his house, and in the backyard, beneath the spreading limbs of the old elm, two little girls turned cartwheels and somersaults before they stopped to look up into the tree.

A couple of pistols, those girls. Considering they'd never had a yard to play in before—he shuddered at the very thought—they seemed to take to outdoor play like a duck takes to water. As he rode closer, he saw Carrie give Amy a boost up into the tree and then scramble up after her.

Trey wondered if their mother knew her daughters were turning into a couple of tree-climbing little squirrels.

She already knew they loved to ride a horse. He'd have to give them another go at it this afternoon. Bareback, this time, he decided. His saddle was just too big for them.

Of course, they would smell a lot more like horse than little girl when they got through, but who cared? It was the fun that counted.

Besides, if he could get Laurie up again, there would be no saddle between them, as there had been yesterday, with her in the seat and he behind on the skirt. Bareback, it would be just the two of them, cupped together like a couple of spoons.

Blood rushed to his loins at the mere thought.

And shame on him for having lascivious thoughts about a woman while watching her two daughters at play.

In the next instant his heart stopped as a shrill scream split the air and Amy fell from the tree.

''Oh, God. Amy.''

She didn't move.

With his heart in his throat, Trey clapped his spurs to Soldier's sides and leaned low over the horse's neck, praying with every hoofbeat.

It took him long, agonizing seconds to reach the backyard and pull Soldier to a sliding halt. By the time he had jumped from the saddle, Laurie was there kneeling at her fallen daughter's side.

"It hurts, Mama, it hurts."

Thank God, Trey thought. At least she was conscious and talking. And moving, he noted. And crying, the poor little thing.

"Let me see," Laurie was saying.

"How bad is it?" Trey asked, kneeling beside them.

"It's her wrist." Laurie's face had gone ten shades of pale.

Trey didn't figure his was any better. Watching that tiny angel fall from the tree had shaved a good dozen years off his life. "Can you move your fingers, Amy? Let us see you move your fingers."

Amy dutifully moved the fingers on her injured left hand.

Trey and Laurie both breathed a sigh of relief. At least the wrist wasn't broken. But they had yet to get a look at it because Amy had her other hand clamped around it tight.

"Amy?" came a tearful cry from overhead.

Everyone looked up to see Carrie hugging a branch about halfway up the tree.

Amy sniffed, then smiled. "I fell outta the tree, Carrie. It was a *long* way, too."

"I *told* you to be careful," Carrie scolded, using her forearm to swipe at the tears on her cheeks.

"What were you doing climbing the tree?" Laurie demanded, her voice shaking.

"Never mind that now," Trey said, figuring this was no time for explanations or lectures. "You just stay right where you are, Carrie," he called up to her. "I mean it, don't move."

"Okay, Mr. Trey. But I wanna come down."

"I'll come get you as soon as we see to this littlest squirrel, here." To Amy he said, "Let go now, so we can see how bad you hurt your wrist."

"I'm scared to look." Fresh tears started down her scratched and dirty cheeks.

"Then don't," he told her gently. "Squeeze your eyes shut so you can't see, then take your hand away. Okay?"

Sniff. "Okay." Doing as she was told, Amy squeezed her eyes shut as tightly as she could, and held her breath for good measure.

"Now let go, baby," Laurie encouraged, her voice not quite steady. "Let me see your wrist."

After one long moment and a tiny whimper, Amy finally removed her hand. Her left wrist was red and already looked swollen to Laurie's eyes, but this was new territory for her. Neither of her girls had ever had more than a skinned knee until now.

"What do you think?" She looked up at Trey.

"It's probably just sprained," he told her. "But we should take her in and have it X-rayed to be sure. There could be a small fracture or something that we wouldn't want to miss."

"Okay." She nodded. "Amy, do you hurt anywhere else?"

The child cracked one eye and looked sideways at her wrist. *Sniff.* "No."

"Let me check her over before she gets up," Trey cautioned.

Visions of internal injuries and broken bones danced through Laurie's head. "Do you know how?"

"I've got four nephews who are always falling out of trees and off horses." And not one of those accidents had terrified him the way seeing Amy fall from this damn tree had, but he tossed Laurie a wink for reassurance. "I'm an old hand at this."

His hands were steady as he ran them over tiny, delicate arms, legs, ribs, neck, back. Everything felt all right, but suddenly doubts seized him. What if there was something he hadn't caught, like an internal injury?

Obviously such a thing wasn't important to Amy, because she pushed his hands aside and sat up. "I have to go to the bathroom."

"Can I come down now?" Carrie called from overhead.

Trey pushed himself to his feet. "I'll come get you."

"I can do it," Carrie said.

"Are you sure?" he asked her.

"Carrie, don't—"

Trey cut off Laurie's words with a hand to her arm. "Let her try," he said softly. "I won't let her fall."

For a brief moment Laurie closed her eyes, but visions of Carrie landing beside her sister had her opening them again. She supposed she could lock her daughters in a closet to keep them safe for the rest of their lives, but what kind of life would that be for either of them? Hadn't she herself delighted in climbing trees and riding a bike and roller-skating as a kid? Sure, a child could be hurt. Many were, some tragically, fatally. But as far as she could tell, riding in a car was one of the most dangerous activities a person could do.

If precautions were taken, she knew, children could be saved many serious injuries. Bicycle helmets, knee pads.

But for tree climbing? Common sense and a few firm rules would serve best there. She wanted her girls to be children, to have fun, to know the thrill of conquering that tree, finding that bird's nest.

So now it was time to put up or shut up. After today, with what had happened to Amy, it was quite possible that neither of her girls would want to climb a tree again for a long, long time, if ever.

"All right, Carrie."

Trey took her hand and squeezed it.

"But go slow," she added, "and be careful. One branch at a time."

"You can do it, Carrie," Amy called.

"I know." Carrie's face scrunched in a look of fierce concentration.

"I could do it, too, Mama," Amy said, "but my shoelace came untied and I stepped on it."

"I'm sure you could, baby," Laurie told her. "I'm sure both of you can. As soon as Carrie gets down we'll go in the house and put some ice on your wrist to make it feel better."

"It'd feel better if you kiss it."

Every hurt in life, Laurie knew, felt better if it was kissed. She gladly, yet carefully, placed a kiss on Amy's injured wrist.

Carrie came down one branch at a time, with much

coaching from all three of those on the ground. Usually conflicting advice.

Carrie glared at them crossly. "Oh, just be quiet," she told them. "I can get down on my own."

Laurie mashed her lips together. She should scold, she knew. Her daughter wasn't allowed to sass. But Laurie feared that if she opened her mouth, laughter would come out instead.

Besides, the poor girl had a point, what with her mother, her sister and Trey all telling her to do something different, step on this branch—no, that one. Grab there—no, over here.

Carrie made it down on her own. Laurie grabbed her and hugged her hard.

"Later," she said to her daughters, "we'll talk about what you were doing up in that tree."

"It was a bird's nest, Mama." In her excitement over telling about the nest, Amy forgot her injury. She jumped and made a wide gesture with her arm and jarred her wrist and yelped. "Oh, it hurts."

"You have to be careful, baby." Laurie ached for her youngest. "Come on into the house and I'll put some ice on it to make it feel better."

"While you're doing that," Trey said, "I need to see to Soldier." Although it killed him to walk away when Amy was crying. "Then we'll head into town for an X ray. That okay with you girls?"

Laurie looked at him with gratitude in her eyes. "Thank you, Trey."

A man would do a lot to have a woman look at him that way, Trey thought. Lie. Steal. Kill. Tend an injured little squirrel.

* * *

They got Amy to the hospital, where the doctor proclaimed the injury a sprain. Nothing broken except maybe a young girl's pride.

"Humph, are you kidding?" Laurie gave her youngest a mock scowl. "I think she's proud of herself for falling out of that tree."

"The object," the doctor said to Amy as he finished wrapping her wrist in a stretch bandage, "is to stay in the tree until you climb down and land on your feet."

They were sent home with instructions to put ice on Amy's sprain for twenty minutes, followed by twenty minutes of heat and children's aspirin for the pain.

It was way past suppertime, but the only one to complain was Katy. Trey took charge of his daughter while Laurie situated Amy in the living room with a pillow to prop her wrist on. By the time the meat loaf was served, both young tree climbers were showing signs of fatigue from the excitement of the day.

But Amy was willing to milk the situation for all it was worth. After she cleaned her plate she looked up at her mother with a pitiful expression. "Mama, can we please have some ice cream? I think it would make my wrist feel better."

"You do, huh?" Laurie pursed her lips to keep them from curving upward.

"Uh-huh, 'cause it's cold. I can put my wrist against the bowl."

"Well now, there's a plan," Laurie said, giving in.

It would be a miracle, she decided, if Amy didn't fall asleep facedown in her ice cream.

Laurie herself was running on adrenaline alone. She didn't know what was keeping the girls going. Their bedtime wasn't for another two hours, but she knew they wouldn't last that long.

"After ice cream, I'll put a plastic bag over your hand so you won't get it wet in the bathtub."

"Oh, cool," Amy said.

Carrie frowned. "How come she gets ice cream for falling out of the tree?"

"Hmm." Laurie narrowed her eyes and tapped a finger to her lips. "You're right. Okay, here's the deal. *You're* getting the ice cream for *not* falling out of the tree. No." She shook her head. "That's not right, either. Trey and I are getting ice cream for not climbing the tree in the first place. We're just being generous and sharing with the two of you. Providing, of course, that you promise not to climb any more trees, both of you, until I say it's okay."

Carrie frowned at Amy. "I *told* you to be *careful.*"

Trey was too wired to sleep. It was nearly eleven and the house was quiet. Everyone had long since gone to bed. He'd gone, too, an hour ago, but to no avail, as he was still wide-eyed.

The picture of Amy falling from the tree seemed to have been nudged aside by the one of Laurie, the way she'd looked on her way to tuck the girls in, with lines of exhaustion marking her pretty face.

He didn't want to think about her, didn't want to think about her daughters and what could have happened today. Amy had been lucky not to have been seriously injured.

But hell, you had to let kids climb trees, didn't you? It was probably written down somewhere.

God, the thought of Katy growing up and falling out of trees left him cold with dread. How did Ace stand it when one of his boys got hurt?

Maybe it was different with boys, but Trey didn't think he would feel that way. A baby was still a baby. And in his book, a five-year-old was still a baby.

Hell, he was never going to get to sleep if he kept thinking about kids and trees and accidents.

Milk. Hadn't his mother always sworn by a glass of warm milk? Maybe, he thought as he quietly left his room for the kitchen, he'd give it a try. But he drew the line at warming it, unless there was chocolate to go in it. And marshmallows.

The small light over the stove was the only light in the room, but it was more than enough to allow him to see Laurie sitting at the kitchen table, slumped over a mug.

"I thought I was the only one who couldn't sleep." Trey crossed the room and stood behind her chair.

She craned her neck to look at him. "I was just about finished here. Can I get you something?" She started to rise.

"Stay put. You're off the clock." Trey put his hands on her shoulders and pushed her gently back onto the chair. The muscles beneath his hands were stiff as boards. It seemed only natural to massage them. "You're trembling."

She nodded jerkily. "I can't seem to stop. I was fine until I put the girls to bed."

"Delayed reaction," Trey told her. "You've had a tough day."

Laurie nearly melted beneath his massage. "Yeah. Oh, God, that feels good."

"Do I understand that this was their first tree-climbing experience?"

"And the first time either of them has ever really been hurt."

"You're kidding." Trey paused, then resumed rubbing her shoulders. Her skin felt cold beneath her blouse. "How do kids get to be five and six years old without getting hurt? Not that I take it lightly. I'll probably have nightmares about seeing Amy come tumbling out of that tree. But how could this be her first accident?"

"Lack of opportunity, I suppose," Laurie said. "Until we moved in with my parents a few weeks ago, we lived in an apartment. I took them to the park to play every chance I could, but they really never played outside much, and never on their own, until we came here."

"And you're feeling guilty because you weren't out there watching them."

"It's a mother's job to feel guilty when something happens to one of her babies."

"So, if you'd been out there you wouldn't have let them climb the tree?"

"I've asked myself that all evening, and I honestly don't know. I want them to play outdoors. I want them to be normal, active kids, a little rowdy now and then. Carrie, especially, is too quiet, too reserved, since…well, for the past year or so.''

"Am I not supposed to guess that has something to do with your divorce?''

Beneath his hands she shrugged. "Jimmy hurt her.''

"Your ex?''

She nodded. "He hurt both of them, but nothing keeps Amy down for long.''

"So I've noticed. Do they miss him?''

"Even when he was home he never paid them any attention. Jimmy was—is—a master at indifference, at what you might call casual neglect. This way, with him gone, the girls don't have to be disappointed every day when he ignores then. Now they know he doesn't live with us, and they seem to accept his absence.''

"Except that Carrie's quieter, more reserved than you'd like.''

Wrapping her hands around her lukewarm mug, Laurie tried to order her thoughts. Maybe she shouldn't be having this conversation with Trey, but he was so easy to talk with, and she so desperately needed someone nonjudgmental to talk to. Sometimes, she knew, talking through something out loud helped you see things more clearly. She could use a little clarity these days.

"Part of it, I think, is the typical birth-order thing. She's the oldest. She feels she has to watch out for Amy. She wants to make sure nothing hurts her sister. She felt enormous guilt today, but I couldn't get her to talk about it.''

"She thinks she could have stopped Amy from going up that tree? Or falling out of it?"

"I'd say it's more that she thinks if anyone had to fall it should have been her."

"Survivor guilt."

"Right." Ah. Whatever he was doing to her shoulders was sheer heaven.

"And the other part?" Trey asked.

Laurie's mind was going fuzzy. She was still shaking, but not as badly as before, and she was still cold. But his hands on her shoulders felt so good. "Other part?"

Keep her talking, that was Trey's plan. The sexual sizzle he'd felt the night he'd kissed her was right now a warm, low hum. More important to him was the need to connect with her on another level. He wanted to scoop her up in his arms and tell her everything would be okay. That her girls were healthy, that she was a wonderful mother. But he didn't think she was ready to hear those things from him. He might have to settle for just scooping her up.

"About why Carrie's reserved. You said part of it was because she was the oldest."

"Oh, yeah," Laurie said. "The other part, I think, is the typical reaction a child has when her parents split up. She blames herself. Wonders what she did that made her daddy go away."

"Have you talked to her about that?"

"I've tried. I've told her that it was nothing she did, nothing Amy did. Really nothing I did, for that matter, or her dad. There was no one to blame."

"I thought you said he ignored them."

"It's not something I remind the girls of. I don't want to say bad things about Jimmy to them. No matter how I feel about him, he's still their father, and they love him. Warts and all. And that's as it should be. If that love ever gets fractured, it will be Jimmy's doing, not mine."

"Why do I get the feeling there's more you're not saying?"

"I think I'm about to fall asleep in my chair."

"You're still trembling."

"Oh, it'll stop. Next week sometime. Maybe."

Trey chuckled. "Come on." He pulled her chair back from the table and did what he'd been wanting to do since he walked into the room. He scooped her up in his arms.

"What are you doing? Put me down."

"In a minute. We're just going right here." He carried her to his recliner, where he sat with her in his arms. "This way you can fall asleep if you want without worrying about ending up on the floor, and we can get you warm. That will help you stop trembling."

"Trey, let me up. I'll just go to bed and I'll be fine."

"Humor me." He grabbed the handwoven serape from the floor beside his chair and drew it across them, then raised the footrest and lowered the back. "There. That's better. Now, you were going to tell me about mothers who tell their children bad things about their fathers."

Laurie thought about tossing off the blanket and crawling out of the chair. Out of Trey's lap. She thought about it. For at least two seconds. But she was so comfortable, and he was so warm. He made her feel cherished and cared for, and she couldn't remember the last time she'd felt that way.

"Did you say I'm off the clock?"

"I did."

She let out a slow sigh, and with it, whatever slight resistence remained to being held by him. "Every time my parents had a fight, my mother used to bad-mouth Dad to the boys and me. I hated it. She decided that if she was mad at him, we should be, too."

"Sounds rough."

"It wasn't fun. I vowed a long time ago that if I ever had children I would never do that to them. Put them in the middle that way."

"So you won't say anything bad about your ex."

"Not to the girls."

"But they know what he's like."

"You think?"

"Kids always know. I was seven the year Jack came to live with us. My mother never said a word against the old man, but I knew he'd ripped her heart out."

"What do you mean? I thought Jack was older than you."

"He is, by five years. He's our half brother. His mother worked in a bar over in Cheyenne. None of us knew about him—not even the old man—until Jack's mother died and his aunt brought him to the ranch and dumped him here."

Laurie leaned her head back against Trey's shoulder and peered up at him. The light over the kitchen stove was around the corner, leaving the chair mostly in shadow, but she could make out his face. "And I thought today was rough.... That must have been quite a shock to all of you, but especially your mother."

"And then some."

"Since I think Donna would have told me about a murder in the family, I take it your mother let him live. Your father, I mean."

Trey's chuckle was as dark as the shadowed room. "Yeah, but it was touch-and-go for a few months. I don't think she ever forgave him, but she did come to love Jack. As I recall, it was a good thing, too, because he hadn't had much caring from his own mother."

Laurie snuggled her head beneath Trey's chin and let out another small sigh.

The sound of it, so trusting and peaceful, went through Trey like warm honey. He could get used to holding this woman in his arms. In the night. While she slept, he added, realizing she was doing just that—sleeping.

He nuzzled his cheek against the top of her head and let himself follow her.

Chapter Seven

The sounds of a baby fretting and tuning up for a cry came over the baby monitor on the kitchen table and woke Trey and Laurie at four the next morning.

Laurie was the first to rouse. Loath to leave her warm cocoon, she moaned in protest. "Not yet, Katy."

A tiny wail of protest emitted from the monitor.

Beneath Laurie's ear rumbled a deep, sleepy chuckle. "I don't think she's listening to you."

Shocked at the unmistakable sound of Trey's voice, Laurie sprang upright, suddenly wide awake.

Trey grunted. "Easy, there. You're liable to make sure Katy's an only child."

"What are you doing here?" Laurie demanded. Then she blinked and realized she was in the living room rather than her bed. She was in Trey's recliner.

More specifically, she was *on his lap*. "What am *I* doing here?"

"Remember? Last night, the kitchen, the shakes?"

Laurie moaned again. "Oh, God. I can't believe I fell asleep."

"I can." Trey smoothed a hand along her back. "It was a hell of a day."

It was all Laurie could do to keep from arching into his touch with a moan of sheer pleasure. How long had it been since she'd awakened to a man's strong hands stroking her body?

Don't think about it.

Right. This was entirely different. Nonsexual. Platonic, even.

So why was her blood singing in her veins? Why was heat pooling and throbbing low and deep in her center?

"I've got to go." She scrambled none too carefully off Trey and out of the chair.

Trey let out an *umph,* probably due to her placing a hand, and therefore her weight, on his chest to lever herself up.

"Laurie?"

As she moved around the chair to make a bee-line for the hall and Katy's room, Trey caught her hand and drew her to a halt.

"Trey, Katy's awake," she said in a rush.

"Before you go back on the clock…" He drew her hand to his mouth and ran his tongue across her knuckles.

Laurie's knees nearly buckled. "Trey," she gasped. "What are you doing?"

"I just want you to know how much I enjoyed sleeping with you last night."

A bubble of stunned, horrified laughter escaped before Laurie could slap a hand across her mouth to cut it off.

"I'd really like to do it again," he said, his voice going deeper. "For real, next time."

Laurie's breath caught in her throat. What was a woman supposed to say to an outrageous comment like that? For a moment all she could do was stare at him, her mind a blank except for the sudden sharp picture of the two of them entwined on his bed at the end of the hall.

From beyond the room Katy let out a howl. *Somebody! Come change my diaper and feed me. Right now.*

Still unable to come up with anything resembling an appropriate response to Trey, Laurie pulled her hand free and rushed from the room.

Okay, she ran. Katy needed her, after all. She wasn't running from Trey. Certainly not. He'd only been teasing her.

Hadn't he?

What if he wasn't teasing?

Could he have meant it? Could he really want her?

Oh, heavens, what was she going to do with these hot, tingling sensations running all over and through her? These pictures that danced erotically in her head?

This knowledge that he wasn't teasing. That he wanted her. And she wanted him.

"Oh, Katy," she whispered as she turned on the

light and leaned over the baby's crib. "What am I supposed to do with your daddy?"

No matter how much Laurie might have wished it otherwise, avoiding Trey before he left the house for the day was simply not possible. Fixing his breakfast was part of her job.

She supposed that if she were the cowardly type, she could make him a big pan of oatmeal while he was in the shower and leave a note telling him to serve himself. That would give her until lunchtime to gather her wits and decide how to act around him after that remark of his about wanting to sleep with her again—*for real next time.*

Her problem was, the idea of sleeping with him, shocking though it was, was all too appealing, and that worried her. She was too attracted to him. He was too charming, too sexy, for her own good. He was too...overwhelming.

She had no business getting mixed up with him or any man. She had two young, impressionable daughters. She was doing her best by them and didn't need to be distracted by a man looking for a temporary fling.

Besides, considering her track record with men— namely Jimmy...not much of a record—she was better off avoiding men. She was no good at holding a man's interest, keeping him satisfied. And she didn't trust them as a species, on general principle.

It would behoove her, she decided as she warmed Katy's formula, to simply treat Trey's remark as the joke she was sure he'd intended. If she laughed off any future comments, he would take the hint.

If there were any future comments.

Trey hurried through his shower. After little sleep—and what there had been of it on his recliner with a woman draped over him, cutting off the circulation in one leg—he should feel like something the cat dragged in.

Instead he felt energized. Eager to meet the day. He couldn't wait to see Laurie again. His blood was pumping as if he was a teenager in heat.

He laughed aloud at the thought. Teenager, hell. His thirtieth birthday was only a couple of months away. And there he was, a single father struggling to raise his baby daughter.

Only he wasn't struggling these days. Not since Laurie had come to live with him. Laurie and Carrie and Amy.

How did a man manage to get so attached to two little girls not his own when he'd never been around little girls before?

Whoever he ended up hiring on a permanent basis to take care of Katy would probably be an older woman whose children were grown and gone. She would likely be divorced or widowed, although it might not be bad having an older married couple living on the place. A retired couple, maybe.

But a couple might like more privacy than they would get living in someone else's home. Maybe they would bring their own mobile home.

Looking into the mirror for a final swipe with his

razor, Trey grinned at himself. Hell, he hadn't had so much as a nibble on his ad in weeks. Who was he kidding? He had Laurie for now, but she couldn't stay forever.

Which meant if he wanted to get closer to her, he'd better quit dragging his heels.

And he most definitely wanted to get closer to her.

First, however, he wanted to get in a little time with Katy before his day started. He knew Laurie usually changed her, bathed her and dressed her, then took her own shower before she fed the baby. Trey was usually just getting up about then. By the time he had his shower and was dressed, Laurie had finished feeding Katy and was cooking his breakfast.

A man could get spoiled, having an attractive woman fix his breakfast every morning.

He got dressed, then zipped down the hall to Katy's room, only to find the crib empty.

"There you are." He found Laurie in the rocker, Katy in her arms.

"Were you looking for us?" Laurie asked.

Trey had seen them this way, the woman feeding the baby in the rocker, a dozen times or more. It had always been a pleasant sight, one that made him feel good. But this morning the sight of Laurie in the rocker, feeding Katy her bottle, started an ache somewhere deep inside his chest.

Trey shrugged and leaned a shoulder against the doorway. "I thought I'd feed Katy this morning, let you get your shower without having to worry about her."

Laurie looked down at the baby in her arms.

"You're paying me to worry about her, take care of her."

"I never intended you to work seven days a week. You haven't had a day off since you came here. For that matter, I doubt you've had an hour off. We need to do something about that."

Without looking up from Katy's face, Laurie smiled. "This isn't work."

"It is. She's a lot of work, and I'm going to start feeding her every morning and taking care of her myself every Sunday and give you the day off. I'll even watch Carrie and Amy for you if you want to go to town by yourself."

"And just what would I do in town by myself?" She looked up at him and tilted her head. "I'm fine, Trey. I have nothing to complain about."

"I feel like I'm taking advantage of you. And frankly," he said, giving her an exaggerated leer, "if I'm going to take advantage of you, I'd rather it be for something other than taking care of Katy."

"I don't appreciate being taken advantage of," she told him.

"I don't blame you a bit."

"As a matter of fact, I try not to let it happen. As for the 'something other,'" she said with what looked to him like a smirk, "I'll pass."

He might have bought that smirk, but it was a little ragged around the edge. Nerves? He smiled. "You don't know what you're missing."

"That may be," she said, "but I'll still pass."

He might have let the matter rest once and for all if her laughter hadn't been tinged with nerves. She wasn't quite as disinterested as she would have him believe. "Well," he told her, "that's your right."

"Thank you," she said with a mock queen-to-peasant nod of her head.

"My right," he said as he bent down and slipped Katy from her arms, "is to try to change your mind."

Laurie paused. Then gave him the baby bottle. She waited until he backed up a couple of steps before pushing herself from the rocker. With a narrow-eyed look, she said, "Trey Wilder, are you hitting on me?"

Trey raised his brow. "If you have to ask, I guess I need to be a little more obvious."

By midmorning Laurie was still smiling at the affronted look on Trey's face when she'd asked if he was hitting on her. His look hadn't been because he'd been innocent, but because he'd been perplexed that she'd felt the need to verify what was actually going on.

She didn't know why she was smiling. She should be more worried than she was. He really was hitting on her. Gracious. The last man to do that—aside from the teenage checker at the grocery store back home—had been Jimmy, and he hadn't come on to her during the last several years of their marriage. It had been so long, she'd almost forgotten the feeling.

Almost, but not quite. She at least had sense enough to recognize the rapid pulse and heated tingling in her blood for what it was. Lust.

"Mama?"

Laurie blinked and looked down at Amy, standing next to her at the kitchen counter. For one horrified moment Laurie feared she'd said the word *lust* aloud, and was now going to have to explain it or figure a way to squirm out of an explanation.

"How come Mr. Trey took Soldier away?"

Saved by a horse. "I don't know, baby. You can ask him when he comes home."

"Is it because I fell out of the tree?"

"Oh, honey." Laurie knelt before her daughter, and as predicted, Carrie joined them. "No, baby. Why would you think that?"

Amy toed the floor and stared down at her bandaged wrist. "'Cause maybe we wasn't supposed to climb the tree?"

"Weren't supposed to."

"Is that why? Is he mad at us? Are you mad at us, Mama?"

Laurie put an arm around each girl and hugged them. "Of course I'm not mad at you. I'm not growling or yelling or anything, am I?"

Amy giggled.

"Oh, Mama," Carrie said, "you never growl or yell."

"Oh, I don't know," Laurie said. "Remember the time you put my good shoes in the toilet to see if they would float? I seem to remember doing a little growling and yelling that time."

"But we were just babies then," Carrie protested.

"Does this mean you're not mad at us for climbing the tree?" Amy wanted to know.

Laurie sighed. "No, I'm not mad at you for climbing the tree. But you'd never done anything like that before. I wish you had asked me first. If I'd been there

I might have been able to keep you from falling and hurting yourself.''

Amy tilted her head. "How?"

"She would have told you not to step on that little-bitty branch, same as I told you," Carrie complained.

"Listen to me, you two." Laurie squeezed them tight, then nudged them away so she could look into their precious faces. "There are going to be a lot of changes in our lives. Coming to Wyoming was a new adventure. When we go home we'll have a house and a yard of our own, and you'll be going to a new school. A lot of new things will happen to you and around you. I just want you to be careful. And if it's something you've never done before, I want you to ask me about it before you try it. Okay?"

"Okay, Mama." Amy was perfectly glad to promise.

"Yes, ma'am," Carrie said.

"Can we go outside and play now?" Amy asked.

"I'll tell you what," Laurie said. "You stay indoors today and make sure your wrist isn't going to hurt, and if you feel okay tomorrow, you can play outside."

"Aw, Mama." That was as close to a whine as Amy ever got.

"Can we draw pictures?" Carrie asked.

"Absolutely."

Amy's face cleared. "Can we draw pictures for Mr. Trey?"

"Absolutely. I think he'd like that very much."

Amy grinned from ear to ear. "Can we draw horsies?"

"Well," Laurie said, tweaking Amy's nose. "I don't know. Can you?"

"Absolutely."

It should have tickled him, Trey thought, to have two little girls draw pictures just for him, and on one level it did. But if he was so damn pleased about it, why was there suddenly a lump in his throat the size of Utah?

"What's the matter, Mr. Trey, don't you like them?"

"They're—" he had to pause and clear his throat "—they're great, Carrie. I just never had anybody draw me pictures before. I don't know what to say."

"See?" Amy said. "That's Soldier."

"It sure is. And that's you and Carrie on his back."

"And this is you and Mama in this one." Carrie held out yet another drawing.

"We did them for you," Amy said. "So when we go home you won't forget us."

"Forget you?" Trey said, feeling a kick in his gut at the thought of them returning to Utah. "Why would I forget you? I'm not gonna let you go home."

Amy's eyes widened. "Really?"

Carrie rolled her eyes. "He's just kidding, silly." Then, after a frown and a pause, "Aren't you?"

Trey winked. "Maybe."

"They really got to you, didn't they," Laurie said after the girls left the supper table.

"Yeah," Trey said smiling. "God, they're great kids."

"They are," she said softly. "They're the best."

"If I do half as good a job raising Katy as you're doing with those two, I'll count myself a success."

"Thank you. But I think they've more or less raised themselves."

"No way," he protested. "I've seen you with them, guiding them, teaching them, playing with them. You're a born mother. What's Katy going to be like growing up without a mother?"

"It's not the sex of the parent that counts," Laurie told him. "It's the caring."

"Sex?" Trey straightened and grinned hopefully. "Single parents get to have sex?"

"Not this single parent," she said with chagrin. Then her eyes bugged and she slapped a hand over her mouth.

Trey chuckled and shook his head sadly.

Laurie dropped her head into her hands and groaned. "I can't believe I said that."

"We really ought to do something about it." Finished eating, he pushed his plate away and folded his arms across his chest. "It can't be healthy."

Another groan. "I can't believe *you* said *that*."

"Neither can I," he admitted. "I'm usually much more romantic."

Laurie splayed her fingers and peered through them. "Romantic?"

"That's right. You don't think I can be romantic?"

Laurie lowered her hands and gave him a teasing smirk. "Would that be before or after you come in from having worked on the tractor all day and are covered in grease and oil and Lord knows what else from head to toe?''

"Ouch. Okay, so I haven't shown you my romantic side.'' He wiggled his eyebrows up and down. ''Want me to?''

Laurie imagined for one brief moment what it might be like to have Trey Wilder's considerable charm directed solely at her, an all-out romantic assault. She had no trouble imagining what it would be like, how she would feel. But she couldn't, for the life of her, picture herself afterward. Was that because there would be nothing left...because he would have overwhelmed her, and she would have given him all of herself?

She shuddered and shook her head. ''No, thanks.'' Getting up from the table, she carried her plate and utensils to the sink. ''Who's got time for romance these days, anyway?''

"Who's got time?'' Trey said in protest as he picked up his own dishes and followed her to the sink. ''For romance, you make time.''

"With your baby and my two daughters? Get serious.''

When she reached both hands into the sink, Trey moved in behind her and bracketed her with his arms, his chest a scant inch from her back. ''I'd like to,'' he said quietly.

Feeling his heat suddenly surrounding her, Laurie stiffened. ''What are you doing?''

"You said to get serious.''

Another shudder raced through her. ''Trey.''

He nuzzled his nose against the side of her neck. "I know you feel it, too."

Laurie's mind was going blank. "Feel what?"

"The energy, the heat. The electricity that snaps in the air when we get close to each other. I know you feel it."

Her knees were going weak. "Trey."

"Turn around, Laurie, and I'll show you what I mean."

"Trey, I don't—"

"Turn around," he whispered.

Somehow, for some unknown reason, she found herself turning, reaching, sliding her arms around his neck. She didn't wait for his next move. He had teased her and tormented her and made promises with his eyes and his voice. She wanted what he'd promised, and she wanted it now. She pulled his head down and took his mouth with hers.

It was Trey who groaned. He thought. But it didn't matter. Nothing mattered just then except kissing her. He curled himself around her and kissed her back.

He felt her everywhere: her legs were aligned with his; her breasts pressed against his chest; her belly cushioned his growing erection. When he nudged his hips against her, it was her turn to moan.

Laurie felt the hardness that hadn't been there a moment ago. It made her want. Heat and dampness pooled deep inside of her and had her stretching up onto her toes in an attempt to put that hardness against the place where she craved it.

It was the whimper of need coming from her own

throat that brought Laurie to her senses. "We can't do this," she managed, her breath coming in gasps.

Trey lowered his head and placed his hot, open mouth against the side of her neck.

"Trey, stop. We can't…oh…Trey…"

"Not here," he agreed, his own breath coming hard and fast. "Not now. But soon, Laurie. Soon."

"Trey." She braced her hands on his shoulders and tried to push him back, since she was already against the counter. It was like pushing on a brick wall. Except he was warm.

But he got the message and backed up a scant inch or two.

"Trey," she said again. "I'm not ready for this."

He ran a hand up her ribs and stopped just short of her breast, sending her pulse into overdrive and making her breasts feel as if they were swelling.

"How ready do you have to be?" he asked.

"Stop." The word sounded feeble, even to her ears. "I can't do this," she said. "I don't do this. Casual sex has never been my style."

"Casual?" He stepped back and dropped his arms to his sides. His eyes were dark and hot. "Is that what you think this is?"

"Isn't it?" she asked.

"Maybe for you. I'm not feeling all that casual about it right now myself. I want you. I seriously want you."

How was a woman supposed to answer a declaration like that? Her knees were weak, her chest was tight and, lower, she was hot and throbbing. Her mind was slow and fuzzy. All her blood had gone elsewhere. "I don't know what to say."

"I think you already said it." His voice was gentle, as was his touch when he reached up and stroked her cheek with one fingertip. "You're not ready. I can wait. I don't want to push you into something you're not ready for. But I hope you don't mind when I remind you from time to time that I'm ready."

She swallowed. "Remind me how?" Was he going to pressure her?

"Like this." He leaned forward and pressed his lips to hers, touching her nowhere else but her mouth. It was the most tender, yet arousing kiss she'd ever experienced, and it was over all too soon.

"Okay?" he asked.

She swallowed again. "Okay."

He stroked her cheek again. "Whenever you decide you're ready, you just say the word, and I'm all yours."

She had to grip the counter behind her to keep from sliding to the floor like a heated puddle of wax.

"I'm going to go check on the girls." And he turned and left.

It was a long moment before she was able to gather the strength to turn around and pick up the plate she'd left in the sink.

What she had to decide was if she was going to be strong enough to resist him. If she wanted to resist him. She was supposed to resist him. Wasn't she?

Chapter Eight

Finally the Flying Ace Ranch was proclaimed a chicken-pox-free zone. To celebrate, the family was having a cookout Sunday afternoon.

"We usually do it every Sunday," Donna told Laurie over the phone. "But since the boys have been sick, Belinda and I just haven't had time."

"What's that noise in the background?" Laurie asked. "I know it's not a baby this time."

"That's just Belinda, hooting with laughter. I was being generous including her when I said *we* hadn't had time for a cookout. She doesn't cook around here—by popular demand—unless the only alternative is to starve to death."

Laurie chuckled. "And she pays you to talk about her like that?"

"She considers it a high compliment. So we'll be

safe Sunday, since I'm doing the indoor cooking and Ace is grilling the burgers.''

Laurie knew plenty of people like Belinda, who didn't like to cook, but she'd never understood it herself. She gained a great deal of pleasure from cooking—preparing a meal to not only nourish the body but to please the palate as well.

If the truth were known, all Laurie had ever wanted to be in life was a good homemaker. She wanted to take care of a family of her own on a full-time basis, turning a house into a home where people loved to come.

Actually the truth *was* known, to Jimmy, because she had shared her dream with him before they'd ever married. He had thought it a wonderful idea, because he was just old-fashioned enough not to want his wife to work. He had promised her that she would never have to.

Naive on his part, to make such a rash promise.

Even more naive on her part for believing it to the point of dropping out of college without earning her teaching degree.

Six months after the wedding he decided he was bored in his accountant's job with its steady pay, so he quit. Real estate, that was for him. Big deals, big bucks.

Big pie in the sky. Pipe dreams. Jimmy had proven himself a terrible real estate salesman. Laurie had been forced to take a minimum-wage job to keep food on the table.

That was when she realized that if her children were to have the things they needed and deserved it was going to be up to her to provide them. She buried her dream of being a full-time homemaker, worked her fingers to the bone and went back to school to finish getting her teaching degree.

She'd been working ever since. But she'd meant what she'd said to Trey the morning after Amy's accident. This job did not feel like work. It felt like…her dream.

"Sounds like you're going to have a good time," she said to Donna.

"We are, and so are you, since you and the girls will be here."

"I thought you said this was a family thing."

"Honey, on the Flying Ace, *family* means *everybody,* and that includes you. We're liable to even have the county sheriff or one of his deputies show up for a meal. Whoever happens to be patrolling this end of the county that day."

Visions of dozens of Wilders and their employees—and the local law enforcement community, no less—threatened to unnerve Laurie. Whatever they thought of her would reflect on Donna, since Donna was her aunt as well as the person who had brought her here to work for Trey. "Are you sure?" she asked, hoping she had misunderstood and wouldn't be expected to remember everyone's name and make a good impression on all of them.

"I'm positive," Donna stated. "You don't have a choice, you know."

That sounded like vintage Aunt Donna. When she wanted you to do something, she didn't take no for an answer. Not ever. If she offered a person a choice, it was "Do it my way, or do it my way."

"I don't?" Laurie asked.

"Not unless you want everybody on the place trooping over to Trey's house to get a look at you and the girls. Then *you'd* have to feed them and clean up after them. Trust me, honey, you don't want that," she added with a laugh.

Laurie gave in, and not too reluctantly. She had to admit she was curious about the rest of the family. She'd been hearing Donna speak of "her boys," meaning the three young ones she took care of—or, as Donna put it, "ramrodded," or "rode herd on," depending on the day of the week and how rowdy the boys were being at the time.

"What should I bring?" she asked her aunt.

"Just your sweet self, and those darling little girls of yours. And if you think of it, you could bring Trey and Katy, too."

"Oh. Them, huh?" Laurie chuckled. "Both of them?"

"Well, Katy for sure," Donna answered with a laugh.

"You couldn't pay me to leave her behind," Laurie said. "But I was talking about food. What should I bring?"

"Not a thing. We've got it covered."

"Oh, no. If I'm included as family, I contribute as family."

"Hmm. Okay, bring your appetite. That's what everyone else is bringing."

"Aunt Donna."

"I don't know what you've got on hand over there," Donna said. "What do you want to bring?"

"I can bring potato salad, or a pie, or—"

"Bring a pie. It won't matter what kind. It'll get inhaled. The only other dessert we're having is home-made ice cream, so that'll be great. Tell Trey to have all of you here no later than two. But if you can come earlier, do."

"Okay, we'll see you then."

Sunday, Laurie thought. She had two days to psych herself up to meet the rest of the Wilders. And to learn how to look at Trey Wilder without having memories of their kiss—*kisses*—make her breathless every time she saw him or drew near him or thought of him....

Oh, mercy, were they going to be able to take one look at her and know she'd developed a terminal case of the hots for her employer?

The weather on Sunday could not have been more perfect. It was a balmy eighty degrees with a slight breeze and not a cloud in the wide, blue sky. When Trey pulled the Blazer to a halt near the rear of a rambling two-story house, three young boys exploded out the backdoor.

"Uncle Trey, Uncle Trey!" they cried.

Laurie was immediately struck by the boys' resemblance to Trey, with that coal-black hair and cocky grin. "They're your brother's sons?"

"Ace's, yeah." Trey killed the ignition and glanced at her. "What's that look for?"

Laurie shook her head. "Nothing. It's just that they look enough like you to…well…"

Trey threw back his head and laughed. "To make you wonder, huh? When you meet Ace you'll see that the boys really don't look all that much like me."

She met Ace when he walked around from the far side of the house as she was climbing out of the Blazer. Trey had been right. Ace Wilder was a slightly older version of Trey, but with enough subtle differences, which were mirrored in the faces of his three sons, to have her sighing with relief that Trey hadn't done something unthinkable with his brother's wife—three times.

Ace introduced himself to her while on the other side of the truck Trey was introducing the girls to the boys.

Ace's lips twitched. "We'll have to see how that goes." He nodded toward the kids.

"What do you mean?"

"Well, either my boys will be nice to your girls because they know they're expected to and because I hear your girls are extremely likable, or they'll turn their noses up simply because they're girls."

He led her around the truck and reeled off a string of names. The oldest boy was Jason, age eight. Then came six-year-old Clay, then Grant, the youngest, at four.

A huge white dog came loping and barking from the far side of the house, followed closely by the most striking woman Laurie had ever seen. Not beautiful in the classic sense, but vivid, with slate-gray eyes and short black hair that turned to fire in the sunlight.

"Boys," the woman yelled. "We're gonna have dog for supper if you don't keep him away from the hamburger meat."

"Come here, Scooter, or Mom'll get you." Jason grabbed the animal's collar.

Laurie braced herself to lunge. The dog was the size of a small sofa, and while the boy was somewhat tall for his age, she feared the dog would merely take off and drag the boy in its wake. But there proved no need for a rescue, as the dog plopped its rear on the ground and gave a sloppy doggy grin.

"Look at him." The woman, whose voice dripped with disgust, propped her hands on her hips. "Acting like I didn't just catch him with an empty meat wrapper in his mouth."

"And that," Ace said with a grin, "is my sweet, demure wife, Belinda."

"Hey, it's the fox," Trey said, calling her by her nickname.

"Hey, number three," Belinda called, using his. "You brought them, finally." She crossed the yard and held out a hand to Laurie. "Welcome."

Laurie accepted the handshake, mindful that this woman was Donna's employer. Whatever Belinda thought of Laurie would reflect on Donna. But there was no reservation in Belinda Wilder's handshake or her smile of welcome. Both were warm, firm and sincere.

More people poured out of the backdoor of the house, and still others from around the corner, the way Belinda and Ace had come. Names and faces swam in Laurie's head.

She met Jack Wilder and his wife Lisa, with her leg in a walking cast, and their nine-month-old baby, Jackie. For being only a half brother to Ace and Trey, Jack looked enough like both of them that the three could have been triplets, but for the slight age differences.

As for Lisa, she had the kind of quiet beauty that Laurie had always envied. And the love in her eyes whenever she looked at her husband or daughter nearly brought a lump to Laurie's throat.

Stoney Hamilton came next. His face was lined with age, but his eyes shone with sharp intelligence and wit.

Laurie learned he'd been the foreman on the ranch for more years than anyone could remember. He'd retired several years ago and turned his job over to Jack, but retirement didn't mean he was finished on the Flying Ace.

"Still have to keep these youngsters in line," he told Laurie with a wink. "'Specially them youngest ones, now that they've got young ladies to entertain today. Why don't you introduce me to these pretty girls of yours."

Amy was eating up all the attention. Carrie seemed to be enjoying herself but was, as usual, quieter.

But Carrie seemed utterly fascinated by Frank Thompson, the ranch's fifty-something horse trainer.

"After chow," he told Carrie, "we'll mosey on down to the corral and have a look-see."

Mr. Thompson's exaggerated drawl and bow-legged swagger broke through Carrie's reserve and had her giggling along with Amy, while Ace's three boys rolled their eyes at Thompson's antics.

Just when Laurie thought she'd met everyone, a car pulled up beside the Blazer.

"You made it," Belinda cried.

This, Laurie determined at once, was the sister, Rachel. She was, in a word, gorgeous. A beautiful, feminine version of her brothers. Extremely feminine at the moment, Laurie thought, realizing the woman was about seven months pregnant. She practically glowed with it.

Lord, Laurie thought. Surrounded by all these black-haired, blue-eyed beautiful people, she felt like an alien. Even Rachel's husband had black hair, though his eyes were more blue-green than pure blue. But there the resemblance ended, for there was no mistaking his Native American heritage.

Their son, Cody, was the spitting image of his father. He appeared to be about the same age as Ace's middle son, six-year-old Clay. Cody fell right in with his cousins, and was introduced to the girls, with Stoney keeping an eye on all of them.

"So," Donna said, slipping her arm through Laurie's. "There you have them. The Wilders. What do you think?"

Laurie chuckled. "I think I'm just about overwhelmed."

"They like you."

"They've only just met me," Laurie protested. Although she did want them to like her. For Donna's sake, she told herself.

"Doesn't matter," Donna said. "They like you."

Throughout the afternoon Trey tried to keep close tabs on all of "his" girls.

Katy was passed around from arm to arm until she put up a fuss. In keeping with his decision to give Laurie Sundays off, he changed and fed her himself, then put her down for a nap in the kitchen with the women.

There he was able to checkup on Laurie. Just to make sure everyone was treating her right. Not that he thought they wouldn't, and if they didn't, Donna could give them what for easily enough. He just felt better for checking.

She seemed to be holding her own with the outspoken Belinda and the quieter Lisa, as well as the sharp witted Rachel. If every few minutes she glanced out the window into the yard to check on her daughters, no one could fault her.

Carrie and Amy were his third center of attention. He wanted them to have fun, but he hoped his nephews and their monster of a dog weren't playing too rough. Especially given Amy's injured wrist.

But all the kids seemed to be having a good time in the backyard. He would just stroll on out there in a minute, just to remind the boys there were grownups around keeping an eye on them.

He headed out that way but barely got past the porch when Jack waylaid him and slapped a beer in his hand. Jack steered him away from the kids and around to where Ace stood ruling over the grill in the side yard.

"'Bout time you came around here," Ace complained.

"You wanted me, you should have hollered. I was only in the kitchen."

Jack smirked. "Yeah, and you would have loved it if one of us had stuck our head in the door and said, 'Hey, number three, what's the story with you and the new nanny?'"

Trey frowned. "What do you mean, the story. There is no story."

"Uh-huh." Jack tipped his head back and swallowed a big gulp from his bottle of beer.

"Pull my other leg, bro," Ace said with a smirk.

"I'd be glad to, if I knew what the hell you were talking about."

Jack and Ace looked at each other for half a second, then burst out laughing. While they were still wiping the tears from their eyes a couple of minutes later, Grady strolled up from the barn.

"What's going on?" Grady asked.

"Love," Jack said with an exaggerated sigh.

Trey figured both his brothers must have had a few too many beers, and he said so.

They both broke out in laughter again.

"Look at him," Ace crowed. "He doesn't have a clue."

"You got that right," Trey said, shaking his head.

Grady chuckled. "I think they're talking about you, number three."

In the act of taking another swallow of beer, Trey nearly choked. *"What?"*

Ace and Jack broke up again.

Jack was the first to sober. "We really shouldn't be making fun of him, you know. She seems perfect."

"And those girls of hers," Grady added. "They're a couple of little sweethearts."

"Laurie?" Trey croaked, his stomach tying itself in knots. "You think I'm—that we're—that she's—"

"Listen to him," Ace crowed. "He can't even talk, he's so far gone."

"Yep." Jack hooked his index finger around the neck of his bottle, then his thumbs on the front pockets of his jeans. "And it's about damn time, too."

Trey didn't know whether to laugh with them, start throwing punches or simply walk away and hope they came to their senses soon. "You jokers are out of your minds."

"Sure we are." Jack's grin mocked him.

"That's why," Ace said with a wave of his arm, "you keep thinking up excuses to go into the house."

"I do not."

"And why you follow her around with your eyes, like a lovesick puppy," Grady added, getting into the spirit of things.

"How would you know?" Trey demanded. "You've been down at the barn for the past hour."

"He knows," Jack said, "because he's got eyes in his head."

"Personally," Ace said as he squirted charcoal starter into the grill, "I think it's cute."

"Oh, you do, do you?" Trey held his eldest brother's gaze while surreptitiously slipping the end of his thumb over the mouth of his beer bottle. They were wrong, of course. He didn't stare at Laurie like a lovesick puppy. He wasn't in love with her. In lust, yeah, well, he could admit to that, to himself and to her, but not to his brothers. They had to pay.

"Yeah." Ace showed his teeth in a Cheshire Cat grin. "I do."

"How about you, Jack?" Trey asked. "You think it's cute?"

Jack rocked back on his heels. "I think it's downright adorable."

Trey nodded, studied the toe of his boot. "Adorable. Grady? You got anything to add?" Not that he thought he could get all three of them, but it was the thought that counted, wasn't it?

Grady ran his tongue along the inside of his jaw. "No. I think they've pretty well covered it."

"But you agree with them."

"Hey, it's no crime to fall for a pretty woman. Happens to the best of us."

"It doesn't matter if I say you're all wet, huh?" Trey asked.

"Nope." Jack shook his head. "You're just blinded by love. Can't see the writing on the wall."

"We're not all wet and you know it," Ace said smugly.

"Well, now," Trey said, beginning to shake his beer.

"Hey." Ace held his hand out to ward off whatever was coming. By the look on his face he knew exactly what was coming. He started backing up.

Trey gave a final shake and removed his thumb, while aiming and turning in a half circle to get the most coverage.

Sharp barks of laughter and bellows of innocent outrage echoed from the yard to the barn and back again. No one was left dry. Even Trey got wet, if he counted where the beer squirted back on his hand and dripped onto his knee.

He had managed to get all three of his tormentors square in the face.

It was the funniest sight he'd seen in a long time, and he doubled over with laughter.

His timing might have been better, however, for as the three were swearing and wiping beer from their faces, the kids came barreling around from the back-yard to see what all the noise was about, and the women came out the backdoor carrying a plate of hamburger patties for the grill, as well as paper plates and other items for the picnic tables placed end-to-end in the shade of a tall cottonwood.

Laurie had Katy strapped to her chest in the baby carrier.

"What's going on back here?" Belinda demanded.

"Dad?" Grant tugged on Ace's arm. "How come you and Uncle Jack and Uncle Grady are all wet?"

"Ah...uh..."

"It was an accident," Jack offered, his lips twitch-ing.

"Hmm." Rachel stroked her belly and tilted her head. "And I'm wondering why it is that this so-called accident didn't happen to Trey."

Trey grinned. "Just lucky, I guess."

"Or quicker on the draw," Belinda muttered, eye-ing the telltale beer bottle still in Trey's hand.

Laurie felt the skin on the back of her neck tighten as Trey's two brothers and his brother-in-law grinned at her. "Is there something I should know?"

Jack opened his mouth to speak, but Trey cut him off.

"No," he said quickly. "Just guy stuff, you know. Nonsense."

Belinda rolled her eyes. "Guy stuff usually is. You got those coals ready, slick?" she demanded of her husband.

"Almost." Ace gave the coals another squirt of fluid, then put a match to them. The resulting poof of flames rated a rowdy cheer from the three boys.

"Amy," Laurie called quietly. "Are you being careful with your wrist?"

"Yes, Mama. It won't hurt anymore, 'cause Scooter licked it. Scooter's the dog."

Laurie nodded. "He licked it, did he?"

"Uh-huh. When we get our new house, can we have a dog?"

Oh, Laurie thought with a pang. The things her daughters had missed. "I thought we might."

"Really?" Carrie's eyes lit.

"Yippee!" Amy bounced and laughed. "We get a new house *and* a dog."

When the kids streaked off to the backyard, accompanied by Scooter, who was in doggy heaven with so many pals to play with, the commotion around the grill settled down.

"So," Ace said to Laurie. "You're getting a new house?"

"Well, it will be new to us. We've always lived in an apartment. This will be the first time they've had a yard of their own. We're all pretty excited about it." *And listen to me,* Laurie thought, *running off at*

*the mouth and telling my life story when all he asked
was a simple question.*

"Is it near your folks?" he asked.

With a laugh Laurie shook her head. "Please, no.
They're the reason we came clear to Wyoming—we
needed the peace and quiet."

Rachel's eyes widened. "*This* is peace and quiet?"

"Compared to my parents' house, it most certainly
is," Laurie stated.

"When do you get to move into your house?" Rachel asked.

"The middle of August, which is when I start my
new teaching job at the same elementary school
where the girls will go."

"The middle of August," Jack protested. "That's
barely three weeks away."

At the reminder that the summer was racing by,
Laurie cast her gaze at Trey, intending to merely
sneak a peek and look away. But he was watching
her, and their gazes met. Held.

Three weeks, his eyes seemed to be saying. *We can
enjoy each other for three weeks. How long will you
make us wait?*

Laurie felt heat sting her cheeks and turned sharply
away. "I'm going to get Katy in out of the sun."

One by one the rest of the women followed her,
and soon it was only the men.

Trey stuffed his hands in his pockets and walked
toward the front of the house. "I'm gonna check on
the kids."

"Trey," Jack called quietly.

Trey stopped but didn't turn around. "Yeah?"

"You're not really going to let her leave, are you?"

They were wrong, these brothers of his. They were out of their minds. He wasn't in love with Laurie Oliver. He wanted her, sure. But love? He'd been in love before. It hurt to have it thrown back in your face. It sucked. It sucked big green toads.

He turned his head and looked at Jack, Ace and Grady over his shoulder. They weren't laughing now. Damn good thing, because he wasn't in the mood to beat the crap out of them today.

"Trey? I asked if you were really going to let her leave."

"Why wouldn't I?" Trey said, then walked away.

Chapter Nine

By the time the rest of the food had been hauled out to the picnic tables, the vultures, as Ace termed the rest of his family, were circling, demanding that he hurry up the burgers.

"You can't rush perfection," he stated.

"But we're *starving,* Dad," claimed Clay, his middle son.

"Yeah, *starving,*" echoed the youngest, Grant.

But finally he deemed the first load of burgers perfect. Nobody got their choice of well, medium or rare; they got their burgers the way Ace chose to cook them. Which was, according to consensus, just about perfect.

Everyone found a seat at the picnic tables except Katy, who was asleep in her carriage right behind Trey.

The food was disappearing, and the conversations around the table were varied, from babies to the condition of the grass up in the mountain pasture to beef prices.

"That's on-the-hoof prices," Trey explained to Laurie, "not supermarket prices."

"That's for sure," Jack grumbled.

"No kidding." Ace shook his head. "Somebody's getting rich off cattle, but it damn sure isn't the rancher."

"It sure isn't," said eight-year-old Jason.

Laurie bit back a smile at the boy's seriousness. It was endearing, even while it was also startling, to realize that all of this would likely one day be Jason's, or at least partly his. At eight years old he was already learning the business of ranching.

Just about the time Jack was commenting that no one from the sheriff's office had shown up to eat, the sheriff himself drove in and parked.

"Hey, Dane," Trey called. "We waited on you."

"Yeah," the sheriff said. "I can see that."

Jack and Lisa's nine-month-old daughter, presently sitting on her daddy's lap, clapped her hands and squealed in delight.

"There's my girl." The sheriff bent and lifted her in his arms. "Are you still my one true love?"

In answer, the tiny black-haired girl squealed again.

"You grab her, you gotta keep her," Jack teased. "At least until I finish eating."

"You just don't appreciate my namesake."

"*Our* namesake," Jack corrected.

Belinda saw Laurie looking confused and explained. "Little Jackie was born in the back of the SUV on the way to town. Dane was driving, Lisa was pushing, and Jack was catching. Lisa named her Jacqueline Dana."

Laurie blinked in astonishment. "You're kidding."

"About the name?"

"No, about the rest of it."

"She's not kidding," Lisa said laughing. "The little she-devil decided to come, and there was no stopping her."

Trey introduced the sheriff to Laurie; the man obviously already knew everyone else.

Laurie took a good look. He stood about six feet tall, the same as the Wilder men and their brother-in-law, Grady Lewis. He looked the same, too, with his black hair and blue eyes.

"I really am starting to feel as if my girls and I are aliens," she said. "Don't you have blondes or redheads in Wyoming?"

"We stop them at the border," Dane told her gravely. "Although there was that one redhead," he said with a sideways look at Trey.

"Old news," Trey said darkly.

With eyes the size of saucers, Amy looked the sheriff up and down. She took in his size and the gun he wore at his hip and swallowed, placing a hand on her hair. Her blond hair. "Do you arrest them?"

"Nobody arrested us," Carrie told her sister.

"It was just a joke, girls." Trey winked at them. "I hear Sheriff Powell secretly likes girls with blond hair."

Dane grinned. "That I do."

"Pull up a seat," Ace invited.

Everyone scooted down until there was room for the sheriff at the end of the picnic bench. Once he had a paper plate in hand, everyone started passing food his way.

"So how goes the crime fighting these days?" Trey asked.

"Around here things are pretty quiet, but up in Sublette County they think they've got themselves a cattle rustling operation going."

The gazes of every person at the table, including the children—not necessarily for the same reasons—zeroed in on Dane.

"For real?" Ace asked.

"Looks that way," Dane said. "We're warning all the ranchers in the surrounding counties to keep close tabs on their herds."

"You won't have to tell us twice," Jack said.

"You haven't seen any signs of strangers sneaking around, have you?" Dane asked.

Ace shook his head. "Just our mysterious grave-yard visitor."

"Come again?"

"I thought you knew about that," Jack said.

"Knew about what?"

Ace and Jack looked at each other and shrugged, then looked at Trey.

"A couple of times a year," Trey said, "somebody hikes in from the south road to the family cemetery and leaves flowers or something on our stranger's grave."

Dane's eyes narrowed. "You have a stranger buried in your family cemetery?"

Trey shrugged and grinned. "Doesn't everybody?"

Laurie was fascinated, first by the fact that, if she was hearing correctly, the Wilders had their own private cemetery right there on the ranch. Second, they had a stranger there?

She didn't want to intrude on the conversation, but if the sheriff didn't ask about the stranger's grave, Laurie was going to have to. She was about to burst with curiosity.

"Who is it?" Dane asked.

"Well hell, Dane," Trey said. "If we knew that, we wouldn't refer to him as the stranger."

Dane rolled his eyes, which spoke to Laurie about the close relationship he had with this family.

"Okay," Dane said. "How did this unknown— man?"

"Man." Trey nodded in confirmation.

"How did this unknown man end up in your family graveyard?"

Trey shrugged. "Stoney found him out on the range one day when we were kids. The guy was already dead."

"What of?"

Trey shrugged again. "Exposure maybe. Did we ever know?" he asked Ace.

"Not that I recall."

"So you just buried him?" Dane asked.

"What else could we do? Nobody knew who he was. They sent wires out all over the country with his description."

"Wires?" Jason asked.

Belinda leaned forward to answer Jason. "It's what they did before e-mail."

"Oh."

Laurie couldn't help herself; she was too curious to wait until the men got all the information out. "No one claimed him? No one identified him, or reported someone like him missing?"

Ace shook his head. "Never turned up anything. So we buried him."

"But why here? Why not in town?" she wanted to know. "I thought a family cemetery would be, well, for family."

"Around here," Trey told her, "family is a relative term. No pun intended."

"The guy was found on the Flying Ace," Ace told her. "That more or less made him our responsibility."

"Ours, period," Trey said.

Laurie cocked her head. "Who else is buried there besides actual members of your family?"

"Number three," Lisa, Jack's wife, said, "you've been neglectful. Laurie's been here, what, three weeks? You should have taken her up there by now and let her see for herself." To Laurie she said, "It's a great place. You can stand there and feel the generations of Wilders and others who built this place into what it is. Even the original owners, who lost this land to that first Wilder in a poker game, are buried there."

Dane Powell finished off his first hamburger and

built himself a second. "And you say somebody puts things on this stranger's grave?"

"Yeah," Ace answered. "Two or three times a year we find fresh flowers and other things on the grave."

"Other things?"

"Once there was a full bottle of Jim Beam," Ace said.

"I remember that," Trey said. "That was years ago."

"Had another one last year," Ace told him.

"You don't have any idea who's doing it?"

Ace shook his head. "We find tracks heading south toward the road. It's somebody with small feet. Sometimes boots, sometimes athletic shoes."

"I don't remember seeing anything in my files about it," Dane said. "Didn't you ever report it?"

"Sure we did," Ace admitted. "But your predecessor never tried to do anything about it." He shrugged. "We're used to it now."

"You want me to look into it?" Dane asked.

Ace thought about it a minute, looked around to his wife, his brothers, his sister. "Nah," he told Dane. "If we decide we want to catch the person, we'll handle it ourselves."

"Okay, have it your way. But keep an eye out for strangers, in case those rustlers head this way. Especially once you bring the herd down out of the mountains. Let me know if you spot anything odd."

"Will do," Ace said.

"Fair enough," Dane said. "Are there any more of those baked beans?"

* * *

"You have a wonderful family," Laurie said to Trey on their way home that evening.

"They have their moments," Trey said.

His remark may have been casual, but his voice was filled with affection.

"Carrie and Amy had a ball. Didn't you, girls?"

"It was the best," Carrie said. "Thank you for taking us riding again, Mr. Trey."

"Yes," Amy piped up. "Thank you a whole bunch, Mr. Trey."

"You're welcome a whole bunch. It's the least I can do for the two girls who drew me those great horse pictures. I even snagged some magnets from Donna so we can put them up on the refrigerator."

"Cool," Amy said.

"How's Katy doing back there?" Laurie asked.

"She's sleepy," Carrie said. "She wants to get home and go to bed."

"I know just how she feels," Laurie said.

When they walked in the door of the house a short while later, the telephone was ringing.

Trey answered. The hint of a frown he'd been wearing all the way home deepened. He held the receiver out to Laurie. "It's for you."

"Is it Donna? What did we leave behind over there?"

Trey shook his head. "It's not Donna." He didn't know what Carrie and Amy's relationship with their father was like, and didn't know if Laurie would want them to know the man was calling. He cut his gaze toward the girls and back again.

"Come on, girls," he told Carrie and Amy. "While

your mom's on the phone, why don't you help me get Katy settled?''

''We can help you change her diaper if you want us to,'' Carrie offered as they followed him toward the hall. ''We know how.''

Laurie's voice carried to them from the kitchen. ''How did you get this number?''

It sounded to Trey's ears more like an accusation than a statement of curiosity. Her attitude relieved him somewhat. He was just enough of a snake in the grass not to want her to enjoy getting a call from another man.

But then, he had no real right to an opinion at all on her relationship with her ex or anyone else. Dammit.

At least she didn't seem pleased to hear from the man.

And Laurie wasn't. *Pleased* never entered her mind when she heard the voice of her ex-husband on the phone. Of the words that she did think of, *dammit* was about the most polite.

''What do you mean, my mother gave you this number?'' She was dumbfounded. But it sounded just like something her mother would do. Dammit.

''No,'' she told him. ''Of course I don't mind you knowing where the girls are. But how was I supposed to tell you when you moved out of your apartment and had your phone disconnected months ago?'' She'd tried for two weeks to track him down last spring to remind him of Carrie's birthday, because she knew he never remembered either girl's birthday.

"Your mother didn't have any trouble finding me."

"Well then, she's a better bloodhound than I am," Laurie muttered.

"You can't fool me, Laurie, I know you too well. You were trying to hide my daughters from me."

"Hide them," she cried. "Oh, Jimmy, I'd tell you to grow up, but it's more than obvious by now that you never will."

"If you're not trying to hide them from me, then what the hell are you doing in Wyoming, of all places, and why are you mad because your mother gave me your number?"

"I took a temporary job up here, if you must know, because raising two daughters is expensive. I buy them new clothes, and the next thing I know, they've outgrown them. Funny how that works, isn't it? I guess if I didn't feed them, they wouldn't grow. But then they'd complain. What's a mother to do?"

"Very funny. Who was that man who answered the phone? Are you shacking up with some cowboy up there in the wilds of Wyoming?"

Laurie bit back a groan. "He's my boss. It's his phone number my mother gave you. That's why I don't appreciate her giving it out."

"Put the girls on," Jimmy said. "I want to talk to them."

"What are you going to say to them, Jimmy? What are you going to say to Carrie when she asks why you forgot her birthday?"

"God, were you always such a nag? No wonder

we got divorced. I'll get her something and send it to her. Now put her on.''

"I'll go get them," she said, knowing the girls would be thrilled to talk to him. "But if you hurt them, so help me, I'll make you sorry."

"When have I ever hurt either of them?" he protested.

"Every time you forget a birthday or Christmas. Every time you promise to call or come by and don't. Every time they go months without hearing from you, thinking that means you don't love them anymore."

"Of course I love them, Laurie," he wheedled. "They're my babies. I wanna talk to them."

She told him to hold on, and put the receiver down on the counter, then went to find the girls.

They were with Trey in Katy's room, giving him advice on diaper changing.

"Girls," she said, "your daddy's on the phone."

"Now? But Mama," Amy protested, "we're right in the middle of changing Katy's diaper."

"I'll help Trey do that," Laurie said.

"Come on, Amy." Carrie took her sister by the hand. "We gotta talk to him."

Well, Laurie thought, as Amy reluctantly let Carrie lead her down the hall, so much for them being thrilled to talk to Jimmy. If she were the spiteful sort, she would be glad they weren't eager to talk to him. But she wasn't spiteful. Not usually, anyway. It hurt her to see their ambivalence toward the one man on earth they should adore.

"You all right?" Trey asked her.

"It's not me I'm worried about," she said ruefully.

"It's them. Don't get me wrong, Jimmy's a lousy father and always has been. But it doesn't seem right that there's so little between the girls and him. They're so young, and I've tried so hard not to poison their minds against him."

Trey peeled the tape off first one tab then the other and secured the diaper in place. "Don't beat yourself up about it. Kids are always sharper than we give them credit for. And more resilient, too, if we don't get in their way. From what I see, those are two of the most well-adjusted girls around."

Laurie smirked. "From what you see, those are the *only* girls around. But thank you," she added sincerely. "You're a nice man, Trey Wilder."

Trey winked at her. "That's what all the women tell me."

She laughed, as she was meant to. Then she sobered. "No, I mean it. Here you are, listening to my problems, when you've got falling beef prices, cattle thieves in the next county and a trespasser in your cemetery."

"Just everyday life on the ranch." He stuffed Katy's tiny arms through the short sleeves of a miniature T-shirt, then tugged the hem down over her little belly. "There you go, sweet pea."

"You're so good with her, like you've been taking care of babies all your life."

"Oh, God," he said with an exaggerated shudder. "You should have seen me the first week or two. I was afraid I was going to break her, or cause her some kind of emotional trauma that would scar her for life."

"Who was it who told me kids are resilient?"

"Yeah, well, she's not a kid yet," he said. "She's just a baby."

"And she doesn't know if you do something wrong. All she knows is that you love her, keep her warm and fed and comfortable. And you do it very well. I've never known another father who loved his daughter so much."

Trey didn't know whether to stick his chest out and pound on it in pride, or turn his head away so Laurie wouldn't see the flush he was sure was staining his cheeks at her praise. Or weep because he felt so damned inadequate about raising a baby girl to womanhood. What did he know about being a woman? How was Katy to find her way in the world with only him to guide and teach her?

"How do you do it?" he said.

"Do what?"

"Raise children alone. The single-parent thing."

When she smiled, her eyes were sad yet somehow brave. "One day at a time. Sometimes one minute at a time. And my next minute is to go back in there and deal with their father."

Laurie turned and went back to the kitchen just as Carrie finished speaking with her father and handed the phone to Amy.

Trey stood over Katy's crib and watched Laurie head back to the kitchen.

He admired her. It was an odd feeling. He was a man raised with a strong, healthy respect for his fellow man, and for women. But there were few women outside his own family that he could say he truly admired. None that he'd ever had a close relationship with.

Not that he had a close relationship with Laurie, he thought with chagrin.

"What do you think, sweet pea?" he asked his daughter. "Am I out of my mind for wanting a woman who plans to go home in three weeks?"

And then there was that other question, the one Jack had asked him earlier, before lunch.

Was he really going to let her go?

Chapter Ten

When Carrie and Amy finished talking to their father, Laurie took the phone again and caught him before he hung up.

"I wanted you to know," she said, "that we'll be here another two or three weeks. If you want to call the girls again, the best time is a weekday morning."

"All right," Jimmy said.

"So, what day shall I tell them you'll call?" Oh, that would make him mad, she knew. He hated to be put on the spot.

"Looks to me like I need to be calling every day," he said heatedly. "What the hell is going on up there? Riding horses? Falling out of trees? How bad was Amy hurt?"

Laurie rolled her eyes at the ceiling. "What did she tell you?"

"She said she sprained her wrist."

"That's what she did."

"My God, woman, she could have been killed."

"Girls," she said to the two little faces watching her with eagle eyes. "Go wash your face and hands in the bathroom."

"Can I take off my bandage?"

"All right. And get your hands clean with soap this time, both of you, instead of wiping the dirt off on the towel," she called after them as they trooped down the hall.

"Oh, Mama," Amy called back, "you're such a kidder."

Laurie bit back a laugh, but heard from down the hall that Trey let his loose. Where *did* kids come up with these expressions?

"Are you going to answer me?" Jimmy said in her ear.

"I don't recall you asking me a question."

"You're letting those girls run wild up there. The next time they might not be so lucky to end up with just a sprain."

"You're right, of course," Laurie said. "I'll lock them in the closet until they're twenty-one so nothing can happen to them. Don't you *dare* tell me how to take care of my daughters," she hissed. "You didn't want them. You didn't want to help raise them."

"I have rights."

"You have *nothing* when it comes to them that I don't grant you. Not as long as you choose not to pay child support."

Laurie gritted her teeth and made herself take three

slow, deep breaths. She wasn't handling this right. She had to give Jimmy the benefit of the doubt on this one. She remembered how terrified she'd been hearing Amy scream, seeing her lying in a small heap beneath that tree. Jimmy had never heard of one of the girls being hurt before, because they hadn't been. Amy's blithe news had scared him, that was all. He was merely taking it out on her. There was no reason she had to reciprocate.

"Oh," he said, "so that's what this is about. You want money."

"What *what* is about?" Laurie struggled to keep from shouting. She didn't want the girls to hear her arguing with him. Besides, there was no reason to raise her voice. "You called here, remember?"

"Yeah, but I'll bet you knew I would. I bet you put your mother up to giving me the phone number just so I'd call and you could badger me for money."

Calm. She would stay calm. "Jimmy, say good night and hang up now."

"Why?"

"Because that's what I'm going to do. Good night, Jimmy." She hung up the phone.

Trey found her there a moment later with her hands on the receiver where it rested in its cradle, her forehead pressed against her hands.

"Everything all right?" he asked.

Laurie groaned and raised her head. "As all right as usual after having to go through one of those conversations."

Trey studied her face and feared he might need to revise his earlier thought that she had no feelings left for her ex-husband. There were plenty of feelings etched across her face just now.

"He gets to you, huh?"

She sighed and turned away from the phone. "He knows all the buttons to push. He makes me crazy."

"Look, I know it's none of my business, but it seems to me that if you react this strongly to talking to him on the phone, there must be some feelings left between the two of you."

"Feelings?" She nearly laughed. "Oh, yeah. They run the gamut."

Trey felt a sinking sensation in the pit of his stomach.

"Animosity, indifference, mistrust, disappointment. Yeah, we've got feelings between us. And those are just mine. His are a lot more volatile."

"Does he want you back?"

Laurie saw the uncertainty in Trey's eyes. He'd been coming on to her for days, and now he was wondering if her feelings for Jimmy were the reason she kept pushing him away. He couldn't be more wrong, but should she tell him that? Wouldn't this be the best way to make sure nothing happened between the two of them during the short time she had remaining on their agreement?

"Or maybe I should ask if you want him back," Trey said quietly.

From down the hall came the sounds of running water and laughing girls.

"I should let you think that," Laurie told him. "It would simplify things between us."

"Would it?" He advanced on her.

Laurie held her ground. "If you thought I still cared for Jimmy, you'd quit coming on to me."

He took another step. "Would I? Or would I do my damnedest to make you forget him?"

Now he was making her nervous. "Trey, stop it."

"Why? You've as much as told me you don't have feelings for him. Why should I stop?" His voice lowered, turned to velvet. "Why should you stop me, when you know you don't want to?"

Laurie's emotions were about to seesaw for yet another time this day. She could feel herself weakening. She'd spent the day amid the chaos of a large, loving family, argued with her ex-husband, worried about her daughters, and now all she wanted to do was give in to Trey's dark voice and steamy promise and shut off her mind with hot, meaningless sex.

But she'd never had meaningless sex in her life. It simply wasn't in her to have sex for the sake of having sex.

She wasn't altogether certain she'd ever had what could be termed *hot* sex, either.

But if she gave in to Trey, the act would be hot, she was sure, and it would not be without meaning. Not with him. She cared too much for him. She greatly feared her heart was at risk. If she made love with him, she would be surrendering part of herself, and she could not afford to lose any more pieces. She'd lost more than enough of her self-respect, her courage, her independence to a man once, and had only recently regained those missing parts of herself. She wasn't ready to surrender anything to anyone.

"I told you I wasn't ready," she said to him. If her

voice came out harsher than she intended, that was all right with her. Let him think she was angry with him.

Trey heard the harshness in her voice and assumed it was anger. Justifiable anger, he admitted. But he knew he could still change her mind. Without much effort he could have her in his bed, where he'd wanted her for days and days.

But it wasn't only her anger or the little girls down the hall that caused him to back off. It was a cold dash of reality.

What the hell did he think he was doing, pressuring her this way? He'd lost all common sense. She was making him crazy was all he could figure.

He scrubbed a hand down his face. "Do me a favor. The next time I get out of line, just pick up a heavy skillet and conk me on the head."

Laurie knew that if she laughed, all her efforts would have been wasted. She was safer, much safer, if he thought she was angry. So she merely nodded, then said she was going to check on the girls.

Because the day at headquarters had been so exciting, there was no way Laurie could convince the girls to go to bed early, no matter how tired they were.

She was a little concerned that neither of them mentioned their father all evening. Instead they talked about the four young boys they'd met, Jack and Lisa's baby, Aunt Donna and the sheriff with his badge, his gun and those cool handcuffs on the back of his belt.

But finally, thirty minutes past their usual bedtime, Laurie had them bathed and in bed.

"How's your wrist?" she asked Amy.

Amy held up her unbandaged wrist. "It's okay as long as I don't bump it."

"Do you want me to put the bandage back on?"

"No."

"You're sure? Maybe just for tonight?"

"Nah, I'm just gonna go to sleep, so I won't be bumping it."

"All right, then. But if it hurts in the night, you come and get me, okay?"

"Okay."

Laurie heard their prayers and kissed them goodnight, but before she could turn out the light and leave, Carrie stopped her.

"Mama?"

"What, honey?"

"Do you want us to tell you what we talked about with Daddy?"

Laurie's stomach tightened. "Only if you want to tell me."

Carrie shrugged, and Amy copied her.

"We just talked," Amy said. "That's all."

"Okay," Laurie said. "That's fine, then."

But Carrie wasn't ready to let the subject go. "Can I ask you a question?"

"Well, of course you can." Laurie sat on the side of the bed and smoothed the hair from her elder daughter's face. "What is it?"

"It's…it's about Daddy."

The knot in Laurie's stomach twisted tighter. "What about him?"

Carrie hesitated and looked away.

"Come on, honey, you know you can ask me anything. Did he say something that upset you?" Oh, damn, she shouldn't put thoughts like that in the girls' heads. If they were upset, they sure hadn't shown it. Until now, with Carrie's hesitation.

"How come Daddy lies?"

The knot in Laurie's stomach turned to ice. "What do you mean? What makes you think he lied?" *I'll kill him,* she thought. *I'll cut out his tongue and throw it down the garbage disposal and then I'll hang him by his heels until he dies.*

Carrie shrugged and picked at a thread on the blanket. "He said that if you hadn't brought us to Wyoming, he would have come to see us this weekend and taken us to the zoo."

"And bought us cotton candy," Amy added.

"But he wouldn't have come, would he, Mama?" Carrie asked. "Not really."

Laurie's heart ached. She had done her best to keep from tarnishing her daughters' affection for their father. Now, it seemed, he was going to destroy it himself. No matter how she felt about Jimmy, she didn't want the girls to think badly of him. She truly didn't. They should be able to love their own father with a full and free heart. Whatever she said now, she needed to weigh her words carefully. Because while she didn't want them to stop loving Jimmy, she would not allow herself to be caught lying for him, either, because then her girls would not trust her.

Finally she said, "I don't know, honey. He might have."

Carrie shrugged. "Maybe."

"But we're glad we came to Wyoming," Amy said with her irrepressible grin.

"Yeah, Mama, we're glad," Carrie confirmed.

Laurie smiled at both of them. "Me, too. Now how about some sleep, okay?"

"Okay," Carrie said.

"Mama?" This time it was Amy, and she wasn't grinning now.

"What, baby?"

"Is it okay to still love Daddy, even if he doesn't always tell the truth?"

"Oh, baby." Laurie pulled both girls to her chest, to her heart, and held them close. "You can always love your daddy, no matter what. He's your daddy, and that's what little girls do with daddies, they love them. It doesn't matter what they do, it's still okay. Okay?"

Both girls wiggled out of her arms and flopped down on the bed.

"Okay." Amy's grin was back.

Laurie made it all the way to the door again.

"Mama?"

Laurie bit back a grin. "What, Amy?"

"Is it okay if we love Mr. Trey?"

"Oh, sweethearts." She lowered herself to the edge of the bed again. "You can love anybody you want. Of course you can love Mr. Trey and Katy and—"

"And Soldier, too?"

"And Soldier, too."

"We won't run out if we love too many people?"

"Run out of love?" Laurie smiled. "No, you'll never run out of love. The truth is, you can't really decide who you're going to love or why. It just happens. One day, you just feel it.''

Carrie tilted her head and studied her mother. ''Can you make it stop?''

''You mean can you decide to stop loving someone?''

''Uh-huh.''

''I don't think it works that way. It can stop on its own, without you even realizing it, but you can't just decide you're not going to love someone. That won't stop the feelings inside you.''

''Is that what happened to you and Daddy? The love just stopped?''

''I'm afraid so, honey. It wasn't something either one of us made happen.'' Well, that wasn't entirely true. Laurie might not have been able to stop herself from loving Jimmy, but his actions could make the feelings dry up quickly enough. *He* could make her stop loving him. Could and did.

''Oh.'' Carrie might have said more, but a big yawn stopped her.

''I'm going to turn out the light now,'' Laurie said, rising from the bed. ''You two go to sleep.''

''Okay,'' Carrie said. ''G'night, Mama.''

''Good night, honey.''

''G'night, Mama,'' Amy echoed.

''Good night, baby.''

''Mama?''

''What, Amy?''

''I'm not a baby anymore, you know.''

Laurie smiled and turned out the light. ''I know. But don't be mad if I still call you that, okay?''

''Okay.''

* * *

When Laurie finished cleaning up the bathroom—
a disaster area after the girls' bath—she heard Katy
fussing and went to check on her. Trey was already
there.

"Does she need changing?" Laurie asked.

"No, I think she just needs holding. I think she got
a little spoiled today."

"Do you want me to take her?" Laurie asked.

"No, thanks, I've got her." And so saying, he
lifted Katy into his arms. "Listen, Laurie, about earlier."

"Let it go, Trey."

"No, I owe you an apology."

"For what?" she asked. "For coming on to me
again?"

"My timing could have been better."

"Or you could have not done it at all," she suggested.

"No." He soothed a hand over Katy's back. "I
guess I can't help that, but I should have backed off
the first time you said to."

"Yes," she told him, turning to leave the nursery.
"You should have."

Distance, Laurie decided as she lay in bed that
night unable to sleep. Distance was the key. If she
could keep enough distance—emotional as well as
physical—between herself and Trey, they could get
through these last three weeks without doing something that she, if not both of them, might regret.

It's not the things you do in life that you grow to regret, it's the things you don't do.

"Oh, shut up," she muttered to that smug voice in the back of her head.

The next morning Laurie served Trey his breakfast, then headed out of the kitchen.

"You're not eating?" he asked, noting the single place setting at the table, as well as her hasty exit.

"I'm eating with the girls today. Excuse me. I want to get the first load of laundry started."

Trey bit the inside of his jaw as she fled down the hall. He must have blown it worse than he'd thought last night for her to be so blatantly obvious about avoiding him.

Dammit, he had to find a way to make it up to her. Above all else, he valued her friendship and didn't want to lose that just because he had a bad case of the hots for her.

Laurie stopped in the middle of the hall. This was the day she wanted to wash all the bedding, but she somehow could not make herself walk into Trey's bedroom and stand over his bed, touch his sheets, while he was just down the hall. It suddenly seemed too intimate an act. Which was ridiculous, she knew, but there it was, the idea of bed sheets and intimacy, and there was no getting it out of her head.

"Idiot," she called herself as she turned and entered her own bedroom. There she had no trouble stripping the bed. If she was a little rougher than necessary, well, no one was watching, were they?

Lord, she needed to get her head on straight. And she needed to make a trip to town to the grocery store that afternoon, too. She would wait until after lunch. That way, if she was gone longer than she planned, no harm done. Serving her employer a late supper would not inconvenience him the way a late lunch might.

She had to pass through the kitchen to get to the laundry room with the first load of sheets, but Trey was at the sink rinsing his dishes, so she wasn't sure if he even knew she was there. She was back in her room putting clean sheets on the bed when she heard the backdoor. It didn't exactly slam, but it certainly shut firmly.

Laurie sniffed. What did he have to be mad about? She was the one being pressured, wasn't she?

But the truth was, the only person really pressuring her was herself.

The admission was an eye opener. Was she pressuring herself to say no when she wanted to say yes?

"Idiot."

"Who you talking to, Mama?"

At the sound of Amy's voice from the doorway, Laurie stifled a shriek. Her heart knocked hard against her ribs. "Baby, what are you doing up this early?" It wasn't quite seven, and the girls never woke before eight on their own.

"My wrist hurts." She held up the offending part and cradled it in her other hand. "I musta bumped it in my sleep."

"Oh, poor baby. Come on, let's put your bandage back on and give you some aspirin. Will that help?"

Groggy and still half asleep, Amy nodded.

"We have to go to town today for groceries. While we're there we'll stop by the hospital and have the doctor look at it, okay?"

"If we have to."

Getting through lunch with Trey was easier than Laurie had feared. Easier because the girls kept him occupied with their endless questions and chatter.

Trey was so patient with them. He seemed to genuinely enjoy their company. He listened to them, paid attention to them, answered their questions in a way that they could understand, and never talked down to them.

Their own father had never been half so good with them. And maybe Trey wouldn't be either after the newness wore off, but she doubted it. She'd seen the way he interacted with his family. He was a family man. He should have a dozen children of his own. Katy was one lucky little girl to have him for a daddy.

There you go again, singing his praises.

"I know, I know," she muttered. "Girls," she called. "Are you ready? It's time to go."

"I'm tying my shoes," Amy called from the girls' room.

Laurie double checked to make sure she had everything she might need for Katy, then carried the diaper bag out and put it in the back of the Blazer.

Soon the girls were ready. A few minutes later, with Katy strapped in between Carrie and Amy in the back seat, they were off on their way to town.

"Do we get a treat when we get to town?" Amy asked.

"What kind of treat?"

"Ohhhh, like an ice cream cone or a Popsicle or a candy bar or something. We're supposed to get a treat."

"Says who?" Laurie asked. This was all news to her.

"Clay says they always get a treat when they go to town."

"Clay, huh?"

"Uh-huh. He's the middle brother. He's six. His daddy's name is Ace, like in a deck of cards. He helped me ride their dog."

"You rode their dog?" Well, Laurie thought, the animal had certainly been big enough to ride.

"Uh-huh. Didn't you see us?"

"I must have missed that."

"Amy likes Clay," Carrie said.

"She does, does she?"

"Of course I do," Amy said defensively. "'Cause he's nice. You like Jason."

"Do not."

"Do, too."

"Do—"

"Girls."

Chapter Eleven

Trey was out on the tractor, in the cornfield about two miles west of the house, and his concentration was shot. Primarily because his conscience was about to eat him alive. It didn't help any that it was hotter than blazes and a strong south wind was about to blow him to Kingdom Come. If he wasn't careful, instead of cultivating the crop, he'd end up plowing half of it under.

The left front tire was a little low, so he would drive back to the house and air it up. While he was there he would tell Laurie that he was backing off for good. That she didn't need to feel threatened or pressured by him.

All the way back to the tractor shed and the air compressor, he tried to think of just the right words that might put Laurie at ease and bring back that sweet smile he'd sorely missed this morning.

Behind and around him the wind blew swirls of dust into the air. Now and then, because he was driving so slowly, a gritty cloud overtook him.

What good was getting her in bed for probably one time, if he never saw that smile again? Would it be worth it?

No. The short-term pleasure was no exchange for the long-term loss.

And that was merely his view on things. What must she be thinking?

She's probably not thinking about you at all, pard.

And if that was true, it might just kill him.

He was forced to focus on his driving, as the front tire was getting lower, the tractor harder to steer.

Finally he pulled up in front of the tractor shed and cut the engine. The sudden quiet was deafening. And short-lived, when, a moment later, he stepped into the shed and flipped the switch on the air compressor.

He started to go on to the house to talk to Laurie while the tank filled but changed his mind. He didn't want to worry about the damn tire while he was talking to her.

He examined the tire and gave thanks that there didn't appear to be any damage. It had always had a slow leak. He should have checked it before heading out after lunch. Next week, he swore, he would take it into town—again. If they couldn't fix it this time he'd have to replace it.

When the compressor shut off, indicating its tank was filled, he aired up the tire.

Then, with his mind made up, he headed for the side door of the house.

It was locked. That was odd. It was never locked during the day. Maybe, being from the city, Laurie had locked it and lain down with the girls for a nap. If so, he decided, retrieving the spare key from above the porch light, he wouldn't wake her. It somehow didn't seem prudent to wake a woman just so he could apologize.

He took off his hat and tried to beat the worst of the dust off himself. Peering at the sky, he wondered if this was just a big wind or if a storm was heading in. So far there were no clouds, but that didn't mean anything. Neither did the fact that it was the wrong time of year for a thunderstorm. They came when they were damn good and ready. Storms couldn't read a calendar and didn't care about inconveniencing anybody.

He pushed the door to the kitchen open and, on a gust of wind, stepped inside. The crackle of paper fluttering—the girls' drawings stuck to the front of the fridge—and the low hum of the refrigerator were the only sounds. All else was quiet.

Yeah, they must be napping. He would just peek in on Katy, then let himself back out.

But Katy wasn't in her crib. Nor were Carrie and Amy in their room. Laurie's room, when he looked there, was also empty.

Trey's heart thumped in his chest. They were gone? Without a word?

He'd pushed her too hard. She'd been upset, maybe even angry.

Angry enough to walk out and go home to Utah?

Please, God, no. But for one startling moment that seemed to last an eternity, his house, his home, felt like the emptiest place on earth.

"Calm down," he muttered. "She wouldn't just leave."

Of course she wouldn't. She'd probably taken the girls over to headquarters to visit Donna. All he had to do was call—and act like he was checking up on her?

His boot heels made a hollow echo on the kitchen floor. Almost as hollow as the sound of his own heart.

He was reaching for the phone when something white on the floor caught his eye.

It was a note: "Gone to town for groceries. Supper as soon as we get back. Laurie."

The small piece of paper must have blown off the table or counter when he opened the door.

He felt like a fool. To town for groceries. Not home to Utah. She hadn't run out on him. He should have known better than that. He shouldn't have assumed the worst. But dammit, she meant something to him. Just what, he wasn't sure, and wasn't sure he wanted the complete and honest answer.

At any rate, his apology would have to wait until later. He placed the note on the table and let himself out the side door, the way he'd come in.

The wind had shifted while he'd been in the house. Now instead of gusting out of the south, it came from the west, sweeping down off the mountains, and it was cooler. Not cool enough to suit Trey, but he figured that would come in the next couple of hours. A few clouds were gathering along the peaks of the Wyomings.

Might get some rain before the day was out, he thought. He'd better finish cultivating the corn.

While Trey was driving the tractor back out to the field, Laurie was at the grocery store in Hope Springs getting an earful of the youthful escapades of her employer.

"Oh, yes, he was quite the character, your Trey was." Mrs. Biddle smiled and shook her head. "Still is, from time to time, but at least he hasn't called lately to ask if we've got Cap'n Crunch in a box."

Laurie mashed her lips together. "He didn't."

"Oh, he surely did."

"Do you?" Amy wanted to know. "Do you have Cap'n Crunch in a box?"

"Well, we're a grocery. Of course we do."

"Then you better let him out…" Amy began with a giggle.

"…or he'll suffocate in there," Mrs. Biddle finished for her. "Lord, help us, she's just like him."

Amy giggled again. Carrie rolled her eyes, but she couldn't hold back a laugh.

"Hear that, Katy?" Laurie said to the baby strapped to her chest. "Mrs. Biddle says Amy's just like your daddy."

"Then there was the time he left a trail of croutons all over the store," Mrs. Biddle said.

"Croutons?" Laurie blinked, fascinated by this new and different look at Trey.

"Why, of course," Mrs. Biddle said. "No ordinary breadcrumbs for that Wilder, no sirree Bob."

"Since you're telling the tale, I assume he got caught?"

"Lord a'mercy, yes. Henry—that's Mr. Biddle, my husband—nabbed him by the scruff of his neck right there in front of the canned goods. Those croutons—seasoned, as I recall—trailed from the bread aisle where he got them, on down to dairy, over to the soda pop cooler, past the meat counter and up the cookie aisle. When Henry said, 'Boy, what in Sam Hill do you think you're doing?' young Trey—he must have been about ten then, 'cause it was a couple of years before their folks got killed in that car wreck on the way back from Jackson Hole. Anyway, he says, 'Heck, Mr. Biddle, this place is so cotton-pickin' big, how else is a fella supposed to find his way back out again?'"

"Your daddy was a pistol," Laurie said to Katy.

Katy was more interested in gumming her fist than in the exploits of her somewhat infamous father.

"I assume your husband made him pay for the croutons," Laurie said when she stopped laughing.

"Oh, yes, indeedy. Then he made that boy call his daddy on the phone and tell him what he'd done. I don't imagine the poor kid sat down for a month of Sundays after that. King Wilder, God rest his soul, wasn't known for his leniency or compassion where those boys of his were concerned."

Carrie's eyes bugged. "Mr. Trey got a spanking?"

"Well, now, young lady, I don't know for sure, but

that's my guess. But he wasn't a mister back then. He wasn't much older than you.''

Laurie wondered if the girls' hero had just been knocked off his pedestal.

''I bet nobody would try to spank him now,'' Amy said stoutly.

Ah, Laurie thought. He was still Amy's champion, after all.

''No,'' Mrs. Biddle allowed. ''Nobody would try to spank him now.''

''Who's been getting spanked?''

''Sheriff.'' Laurie smiled at Dane Powell.

''Mr. Trey, Sheriff.'' Amy looked up and up until her gaze reached Dane's face. ''We think his daddy spanked him when he was little.''

''I wouldn't be surprised,'' Dane said with a wink. ''Are you ladies about finished with your shopping?''

''Just about.'' Laurie had the feeling he was asking for a reason. ''Why?''

''The sky's getting dark out there. Looks like it could storm, and you've got a long drive home.''

''Well then,'' Mrs. Biddle said. ''Let's start checking you out while you go grab whatever else you need so you can get on home.''

Within a few minutes Laurie's groceries were bagged and ready, she'd signed the ticket, and she was herding Carrie and Amy toward the door. She was forced to draw the girls to a halt when a tall, leggy redhead strolled through the door and, with hands planted on her hips, stopped right in front of Laurie.

''Excuse us,'' Laurie said.

"Oh, no need. I just wanted to get a good look at Trey's latest plaything."

Shock froze Laurie to the spot and locked her tongue firmly against the roof of her mouth. For an instant she couldn't understand what on earth the woman meant. Plaything? Was the woman mean enough to call Trey's daughter a plaything?

But the smirk on the woman's face told her the remark was not about Katy. It was about her. Laurie didn't know whether to laugh in the woman's face— considering the state of affairs, or lack thereof, between her and Trey, such an accusation was certainly laughable—or claw the woman's eyes out for maligning her character, and for doing so in front of Carrie and Amy, not to mention Mrs. Biddle and the sheriff.

But Laurie neither laughed nor lunged.

First had been the tension and ugliness at her parents' house, which had sent her to Wyoming. Then an argument over the phone with her mother. Then Jimmy had called. Then the new tension between her and Trey.

This, from a total stranger, was simply too much. But she was holding herself together. She would not rant and rave and scream and kick the nearest wall. But neither would she stand there and take whatever this woman decided to dish out.

Laurie's voice was calm when she spoke. "I'm afraid you're mistaken. If you'll excuse us, we're on our way out."

The smirk on the woman's face deepened. "In more ways than one, if you've been around more than a few weeks. Trey doesn't keep his women long."

Laurie took both girls by the hand and turned away. "Mrs. Biddle, would you mind terribly letting the girls pick out one candy bar each and adding it to our tab?"

"Why, I believe that's an excellent idea. Good afternoon, Cindy," she added tersely to the redhead.

"But, Mama." Carrie tugged on her hand. "The sheriff said there's a storm coming and we should get home." Carrie didn't care for storms.

"We will, just as soon as you get your candy bars. Now go with Mrs. Biddle, honey. Sheriff, do you suppose you could give them a hand? I'd hate for them to grab the first thing they see without looking at everything that's available."

The message in Dane Powell's eyes said he understood completely. He was to drag out the candy bar selection for as long as possible. He nodded in acknowledgment. "Be glad to. Bobby, why don't you go ahead and load Ms. Oliver's groceries in the back of that Flying Ace Blazer."

"Will do, Sheriff," said the teenager on sacking duty for the day.

Dane gave the redhead a final, slow look, then he nodded. "Cindy."

"Sheriff. Don't tell me she's working on you, too. My, my, won't Trey be interested in that."

"In law enforcement," he said to the redhead, "they teach us to make sure we have proof before we make accusations. It'd be a real shame to blame an innocent party, now wouldn't it."

The smirk on the redhead's face didn't abate one whit. She merely waited until Dane turned to follow the girls, then she looked Laurie up and down in a manner so condescending Laurie wanted to scream.

"Oh, I don't know," she said to Laurie. "You don't look all that innocent to me."

"Just hold it." Laurie raised a hand palm out. "You've taken your shot. Now it's my turn. I don't know who you are or what your problem is. I can guess, but frankly I don't care. Not that it's any of your business, but I'm working for Trey Wilder on a temporary basis taking care of his daughter while he tries to find a suitable housekeeper to take over before I go home to Utah in a couple of weeks. Meanwhile," she added, lowering her voice, "if you're smart you'll never, ever let me learn that you've been talking about me again, and most especially not around my children. That was inexcusable. Don't do it again."

"Or what?" the redhead sneered.

"Well," Laurie said thoughtfully. "As I see it, I have two options. One would be the law, since you're slandering my good name and reputation."

"Oooh, I'm scared."

"The other would, I think, be against the law, but I can probably get away with scratching up that pretty face of yours by claiming justifiable violence."

The redhead laughed and looked down at Laurie from her six-inch superior height. "You and what army, sister? He'll never marry you, you know."

Laurie eyed her carefully. "Have you been drinking?" What else would explain this woman's behavior?

"He wouldn't even marry the mother of his own poor little baby. He's already married. To the damn

Flying Ace Ranch. That's his mistress, his wife, his world. You'll never get him to leave it.''

The very idea of Trey leaving the ranch was inconceivable to Laurie. He was part of the Flying Ace, and it was a vital part of him. Asking him to leave would be like expecting him to cut off his right arm. "Is that what you did? Tried to get him to leave the ranch?"

For a quick instant the woman's eyes darkened with pain. Then without so much as a blink, vicious anger flared there again. But before she could start on another tirade, Mrs. Biddle and the girls were back, with Dane herding them toward Laurie.

"We're all through here, Laurie, and your groceries are loaded. I'm sure Cindy's finished, ah, welcoming you to town. Come on." He took Laurie's elbow and steered her around the redhead. "I'll walk you out."

It would have seemed rude for Laurie to pull free of Dane's admittedly light hold, but while she appreciated his help with the girls a moment ago, she didn't particularly appreciate being led out of the store like a recalcitrant child.

Outside, the wind gusted through the parking lot, tossing an abandoned paper cup end-over-end past the three vehicles parked next to the building.

"Thank you, Dane, but I don't need your protection."

Dane's lips twitched. "It wasn't you I was protecting."

Laurie raised her brow. "Oh, really?"

"Here we go, ladies." He opened the backdoor of the Blazer and helped Carrie and Amy climb up into the back seat. Carrie had to climb over the baby's car seat, which had been left strapped into place by the center seat belt.

Then Laurie had to climb in with them to place Katy in her carrier and fasten the straps snugly. Katy smiled and waved her fists.

"Was that a thank-you?" Laurie asked the baby. "Well, you're welcome."

When Laurie crawled back out the door to get into the front seat, Dane was still there.

"Are you okay to drive?" he asked

Laurie blinked. "Why wouldn't I be?"

"I thought maybe..." He nodded toward the grocery store, and she knew he meant Cindy, the redhead. "Sometimes when people get angry, it's not safe for them to drive."

Laurie worked her mouth to keep from grinning. He was so obviously concerned for her that she couldn't stay irritated with the high-handed method he'd used to get her out of the store.

"I'm fine, Dane," she said. "Thank you. While I might be tempted to floorboard it all the way home, my cargo is much too precious to risk."

Dane's smile was filled with relief. "That's what I like to hear. I wish more people thought like you."

Laurie reached for the handle of the front door of the Blazer, but he beat her to it and pulled the door open for her.

"Thanks," she said. "Any word on those cattle rustlers in the next county?"

"Nothing yet," he told her. "But we'll get 'em."

"I hope so."

She climbed into the driver's seat and, after a final farewell, drove out of the small parking lot and headed out of town.

On the way into town they'd stopped by the hospital and had Amy's wrist looked at by the doctor. Amy had sworn it wasn't necessary, that the ice pack Laurie had put on it that morning had done the trick, but Laurie had decided to take advantage of this trip to town, just to be sure.

The doctor had pronounced the wrist healing nicely, and advised Amy to do without the bandage and start using the wrist more, although not to the point of making it hurt.

So they'd taken care of that, bought groceries and had a run-in with one of Trey's old flames.

All in all, an interesting day so far. She couldn't wait to see what else would happen.

Chapter Twelve

The clouds along the peaks of the Wyoming Mountains continued to build throughout the afternoon. It was nearly suppertime when they started rolling down and east, blocking out the sun and turning an ugly gray with a slight greenish cast that meant the possibility of hail.

Trey drove the tractor back to the shed as fast as he dared. If it was going to hail on his crops, dammit, he didn't want to add insult to injury by having the tractor beaten to pieces.

He pulled the tractor into the big shed just as the rain started. It was a hundred yards to the house, but he didn't mind getting a little wet.

What he got was soaked, and then some. First it was big, fat raindrops slapping at him as he shut the wide doors on the shed. He turned toward the house, and after he took a dozen steps, the bottoms of those ugly gray clouds ripped open and drenched him in frigid rain.

He ran. But not fast enough to beat the hail. A few small ice pellets at first. No problem, he thought. He had only about fifty yards to go. He ran faster, his boots splashing through puddles already on the path from rain that came too fast for the ground to absorb.

Then the hail got bigger. And bigger. Ice the size of golf balls pelted and pummeled him, threatened to knock him down. He covered his head with his arms as best he could and sprinted the last ten yards to the backdoor.

Laurie had finished putting away the groceries, had fed and changed Katy and was gathering the ingredients for spaghetti to go with the loaf of French bread she'd bought at the store when the rain suddenly started pounding the roof. Then came the hail. She hoped Trey wasn't out in this. Even small hail could do serious damage, and this wasn't small hail.

In the next instant the backdoor slammed open and Trey barreled in, water pouring off him in sheets.

"Oh, good heavens, Trey, you've been out there in that?"

"Not for long. I was halfway in from the shed before it got bad." After pushing the door shut behind him, he shook like a soaked dog.

Looked a lot like one, too, Laurie thought with sudden sympathy. Then, when he stepped into the kitchen leaving a muddy puddle on her clean floor, she got a better look at him. "Oh, God, what happened? You're bleeding.'' She tore a paper towel from the roll near the sink and rushed to his side.

''What?'' he said, raising a hand to his forehead. ''Where?''

''Here.'' She pressed gently with the paper towel and blotted away rainwater and blood.

Trey winced. ''Ow.''

''I'm sorry,'' she whispered. ''It doesn't look bad. It's almost stopped bleeding. What happened?''

''One of those big chunks of hail got me.''

''Only one? You'll probably have bruises all over your head and shoulders, at the least. Your skin's like ice, Trey,'' she said. ''Go get in the shower and I'll bring you some dry clothes.''

Trey started to protest that he didn't need a shower, he'd just had a doozie of one on his way to the house. But he could feel goose bumps rising along his arms and legs, and suddenly it was all he could do to keep from shivering. A hot shower was sounding better by the minute.

''Okay.'' His nod was jerky. ''Hot shower. But I'm going to drip all the way down the hall.''

''That's what they make towels for,'' she told him.

''Boots.'' Stiffly, no longer able to stave off the shivers, Trey turned back to the boot jack near the backdoor and pulled off his boots. No sense adding mud to the mess he was going to make.

He must have been out in the storm longer than he'd thought, Trey decided, for him to be this damn cold. But a couple of minutes later, standing under the hot spray of the shower, he warmed rapidly.

Laurie quickly grabbed a towel from the laundry

room and tossed it down over the large puddle that had formed beneath Trey when he'd stood still long enough to let her blot his head. Other than that, she didn't waste time cleaning up after him. That could wait.

She rushed down the hall to his room and gathered clean underwear, jeans and a T-shirt. At the bathroom door she paused. The shower was running, so it should be safe for her to slip in, leave his clean clothes for him, gather his wet ones and slip right back out again.

It might have worked. It should have worked. It nearly worked. She opened the bathroom door and peeked inside to make sure it was safe. She could just make out his form behind the frosted glass door of the shower. A cloud of steam rose to the ceiling and water gurgled down the drain.

Stepping into the humid warmth of the room, Laurie placed Trey's clean clothes next to the sink on the vanity. She was leaning down to gather the wet clothes he'd left in a pile on the floor when the shower suddenly shut off and the frosted door clicked open.

It was hard to say which of them was more startled when their gazes met.

"Oh." Laurie's mouth went dry. "I, uh…" Her voice died in her throat as her gaze involuntarily lowered. She was sure it was involuntary. She wouldn't deliberately ogle a naked man. At least, she never had before. Yet somehow she couldn't help but follow the path of the droplets of water as they trickled down his tanned, taut flesh. Down his cheeks, his jaw, his throat. Into the gleaming mat of crisp black hair on his chest. Along arms roped with muscles developed not on a machine in a gym, but from hard, physical labor.

Back up to his throat and over that inviting hairy chest again and down, over a washboard abdomen, and down, along a single line of hair to—

"Oh." Heat stung her cheeks. She jerked her gaze up to his face, but couldn't meet his eyes.

Trey shrugged. "I can't help it. This is what happens to me every time I get near you."

Laurie swallowed. The fingers of her right hand squeezed tight around a wad of wet denim. "It does?" *Idiot. What a stupid thing to say.*

"Every time. You, ah, want to hand me that towel, or would you rather just look?"

Laurie acknowledged the heat racing through her veins and the sudden throbbing down deep inside in answer to Trey's obvious arousal, but the humor of the situation was not completely lost on her. "Gee," she said, fighting a smile, "how long do I get to make up my mind?"

"Or," he added, "you could strip and join me in here. There's still plenty of hot water."

For Laurie all desire to laugh faded, burned to ashes by the heat generated by the pictures flooding her mind. Pictures of Trey welcoming her into his shower. Of him pressing her back against the wet tile. Of first his hands and then his mouth, trailing down her body, feeling her, tasting her, inch by inch.

She cleared her throat and looked down to find herself wringing water from his jeans. "I, uh, that is…" She stopped and blew out a breath. Damn. Just this once she wanted to be able to say yes. She wanted to stand up, fling off her clothes and throw herself at him. Devour him, and let him devour her.

But there were two little girls out there waiting for their supper.

And if that wasn't an excuse, she didn't know what was. In reality, all she and Trey needed was a few minutes. The girls weren't likely to suffer if she didn't leave the bathroom for another five minutes.

"Laurie?"

She heard the question in his voice, and she heard more. She heard hope and anticipation mixed with doubt.

Slowly she raised her gaze and looked him in the eyes.

Trey's breath caught somewhere south of his throat. She was his. Right now she was willing. She wanted him.

But dammit, he didn't want their first time together—God forbid it be their only time together—to be rushed, in the cramped and not altogether safe confines of the shower, with two little girls likely to knock on the door if their mother didn't show up soon.

"Go," he said softly.

"Trey, I..."

"I know. Later." He offered her a smile. "For now, just go." He met her gaze for another long moment, then turned away.

"Oh, Trey, your back."

Trey frowned and looked down over his shoulder, as if he could see his own back.

Without thought to the possible consequences, Laurie rose and stepped to the shower door. "It's covered in red blotches." She placed her fingers gently next to an angry red injury.

Trey flinched at her touch.

"I'm sorry," she said. "Here's another cut. It's still oozing."

Trey clenched his fists at his sides to keep from turning around and pulling her to his chest. "It'll be all right," he told her, his voice sounding rusty.

"I should put—"

"Laurie, if you keep touching me, I'm going to turn around and touch you, and I'm not going to want to stop."

Laurie left her hand on his damp shoulder for a long heartbeat before trailing her fingers down his back, then away. She stood silent for a moment, staring at his broad shoulders, his lean hips, his strong legs. Then, when her heart couldn't possibly beat any faster, she bent and gathered his wet clothes and reached for the doorknob.

"I'll go," she said. "For now." She pulled open the door and felt the rush of cool air. "Leave your shirt off when you come to the kitchen. I'll put some ointment on those cuts."

By the time the spaghetti sauce was simmering, sending a mouthwatering aroma wafting through the kitchen, the storm had rolled on across the rangeland, and Laurie found herself amazingly calm.

When she'd walked out of the bathroom and closed the door behind her, her knees had been about the consistency of jelly. She'd had to stop and brace herself against the wall until she steadied enough to walk.

Even then she'd been shaking so hard that she'd dropped Trey's wet clothes. Twice. And it had taken her three tries to get the can of tomatoes positioned correctly in the can opener.

But sometime during her efforts at appearing calm and normal in case the girls lost interest in the television and came to the kitchen, she had crossed a threshold of sorts. Maybe she had crossed it down the hall in that steamy bathroom while she'd stared at a naked man who had so obviously wanted her.

Not just any man. Trey.

If any man had ever wanted her this much, she hadn't known about it. But this man wanted her. This man who stole her breath and made her heart pound when he kissed her. The man who had such tender consideration for her injured daughter. The man who took the time to let two little girls ride their first horse. That same man who had later climbed on behind her and pressed his hand intimately to her stomach, melting her.

She'd never known a man like Trey Wilder and probably never would again. She was going to take what he was offering her and give what she could. When she left Wyoming in a couple of weeks, she did not want to look back and wonder what it would have been like to make love with the man, *the* man, who so stirred her senses that she could think of little else but him.

She was going to take him as her lover.

He was going to devastate her. She cared too much for him for it to be otherwise. But caring too much was her problem, as would be the hurting that would come. She didn't want to waste what little time she might have with Trey worrying about future pain.

Besides, one time might be all she had with him. That might be all he wanted from her. It might be all she would want with him.

Oh, right, she thought with a silent chuckle.

Suddenly something changed around her. The very air seemed to move, yet she felt no breeze or draft.

Trey.

He was there. Without turning to look, she knew he had joined her in the kitchen.

She gave the sauce another stir, then tapped the large spoon against the rim of the pot and set it in the spoon rest next to the stove. Then slowly she turned.

They stood there, not moving, for the length of one breath, then another. Blue was supposed to be a cool color, Laurie thought. But there was nothing cool in Trey's eyes now. They were hot, so hot she swore she could feel the heat from across the room.

He had left his shirt off as she'd told him to. The soft white T-shirt she had pulled from his drawer and left in the bathroom was now bunched in his fist.

Without taking her eyes from his, she reached for the tube of cream she had placed on the windowsill a few minutes ago. "Sit down and I'll tend to your back."

Without taking his eyes from hers, he pulled a chair out from the table, turned it around and straddled it.

Laurie had a death grip on the tube as she took the

three steps to his side. Swallowing hard, she tore her gaze free of his and watched herself unscrew the cap. She squeezed out a drop of white cream and dabbed it on the cut on his right temple. Then she moved to his back.

"Whatcha doing, Mama?"

Startled at the sound of Amy's voice directly behind her, Laurie jumped.

"Ha," Amy crowed. "I scared you."

"You did. I thought you were watching TV."

"It's a commercial. What are you doing to Mr. Trey's back?"

"I'm putting cream on the spots where the hail hit him. See these red places, and these two cuts?"

Amy frowned at Trey's back for a moment then sidled up next to him. "Does it hurt, Mr. Trey? Mama can kiss it and make it better."

"Can she?"

"Uh-huh. She's real good at it. She made my wrist all better." Amy whirled around to his back. "Here, Mama, kiss this red spot."

Laurie's breath caught in her throat. Her daughter looked up at her with such sincere hope, and Laurie did so want to get her lips on that skin, and really, what could it hurt, with a five-year-old chaperoning them?

"This one?" she asked, touching one slightly trembling finger lightly to the spot.

Beneath her touch, the muscles on Trey's back quivered.

"Yeah," Amy said. "That one first. It's the biggest."

Laurie bent and pressed her lips to the big red welt on his right shoulderblade. She felt him stiffen. "Did that hurt?"

Trey cleared his throat. "Uh, no." No, *hurt* was not the word. *Annihilate* came close, Trey thought. "No. It didn't hurt."

"Does it feel better?" Amy asked.

"Yeah. It feels fine." If he felt any finer, he just might explode.

"Do this one next, Mama."

"All right."

Trey fought against a shudder. Each time Laurie spoke, her voice got lower. Quieter. Breathier. If she was trying to torture him, it was working. One by one she kissed spots on his back he wouldn't have given a second thought to. Now he couldn't get his mind past them. He swore he could still feel her lips at each and every place she kissed, and with Amy directing the process, there were nearly a dozen before Laurie called a halt.

"Okay," she finally said. "I think we've got the worst of them. I think your show's back on."

With a squeal of dismay at the prospect of missing something on the television, Amy raced back to the living room.

But Trey wasn't safe yet. Laurie was at his back again, this time with the cream. It was cool against his skin. Soothing, when he knew he needed to be soothed but wasn't sure he wanted to be. "I think I liked your lips better."

"Did you?"

He wondered if that breathy quality in her voice

was deliberate. He wondered, for that matter, if the top of his head was still on. "Do you know what you're doing?" She was, without a doubt, driving him slowly out of his mind.

"Putting cream on your cuts and bruises?"

"That's not all you're doing." He craned his neck and looked at her over his shoulder. "And I think you know it."

All he could think was that it was a good thing he was sitting down when that knowing, woman's smile came across her face.

Chapter Thirteen

Laurie was never sure how she made it through supper that night. More than made it through; she'd cooked it. Thank heaven she'd had the spaghetti sauce simmering before Trey came to the kitchen, otherwise she would never have been able to vouch for the ingredients.

But somehow they made it through supper, and through Katy spitting up on Trey after he fed her, and through Carrie and Amy's bath, followed by just a few more minutes of television, then another drink of water, then a trip to the bathroom for one. Then the other. Then getting Katy settled down for the night. Until finally the house was quiet.

Laurie slipped into her bedroom without saying anything to Trey. Her emotions had run the gamut this day, and she wanted to settle herself.

She'd been amused by Mrs. Biddle's stories about Trey in his misspent youth. Then the confrontation with the lovely, red-haired Cindy. Concern for Trey when he'd come in from the storm. And after that, everything floated in a haze, because her mind and body had been preoccupied with sex.

There. She had actually let the word form in her mind. She was going to have sex with Trey.

But, oh, she hoped it was more than that. She wanted, for this one night, to make love and be made love to. She wanted caring and consideration and red-hot passion.

She might be setting herself up for disappointment, but, well, she'd been disappointed before, hadn't she? Nothing ventured, nothing gained, and all that.

Looking in the mirror over her dresser, she wished she had a slinky black nightgown to wear for him. Or a red-is-the-color-of-fire teddy.

"'If wishes were horses...'"

What she had was blue jeans and a shirt, and beneath them, plain white cotton underwear.

"Listen to me," she thought with disgust. Being a red-blooded male, Trey would surely appreciate the black or red come-hither wear, but he wasn't so shallow that he would care that she didn't have them to wear. And if he was, he wasn't the man for her.

"But he is the man for me," she told her reflection. "At least for tonight."

And it was time for her to let him know it, in no uncertain terms.

Trey lost count of the number of times he had paced the living room since Laurie had disappeared into her bedroom. Was she coming out again or had she changed her mind?

No. He couldn't believe that the woman who'd been giving him those hot, smoldering looks all night had suddenly turned timid. There had been nothing timid about the way she'd looked at him in the shower or the way she'd kissed the bruises on his back or the way she'd met and held his gaze down the length of the table at supper. That woman wanted him, maybe almost as much as he wanted her.

Unless she'd been acting. Teasing.

But why would she? Laurie wasn't like that. She was warm and open and honest.

Dammit, where was she? He was about to go out of his mind. He'd wanted her practically from the day she'd arrived, and tonight everything she did and said had told him she wanted him, too. That she was ready to take this step with him.

At the end of the living room he turned for the hundredth time toward the doorway to the hall, and there she stood. Her name came out on a sigh of breath.

When Laurie heard it, her blood thickened, her heartbeat slowed, then raced. "I said, before, that I wasn't ready."

He walked toward her until he stood a mere two feet away. "And now?"

Nerves suddenly assailed her. Not that she wanted to back out, because she didn't. But she wanted them both to enjoy what was to come, and she wasn't sure she knew how to make that happen. During her marriage, sex had been infrequent and hurried. Since her divorce, it had been nonexistent.

But, looking at this man before her now, she knew she had nothing to worry about. He was a man who knew how to pleasure a woman; she was sure of it. He would make up for whatever she lacked. She only hoped she didn't disappoint him.

"And now," she told him quietly, "I'm ready."

She thought he might kiss her then, but instead, he picked up the baby monitor from the occasional table beside the door, then took her by the hand. Unhurried, as if they had all the time in the world, he led her down the hall to his bedroom.

The lamp beside the bed was burning, and the sheet and blanket and comforter were turned down.

He'd readied the room for her. It might have made her nervous, but instead it made her smile, because she thought it was sweet.

Behind her, Trey closed the door. She heard the faint snick of the lock and turned to him.

He took the three steps that separated them and stood before her. His stockinged feet made swishing sounds across the carpet. He set the baby monitor on the nightstand and took her hands in his. "I've pictured you here."

Laurie gazed up into his face and let out the breath she hadn't realized she was holding. "I've pictured myself here."

"I'm glad you're finally here." He lowered his head and nibbled along her cheek.

"So am I." At the feel of his warm breath against

her face, his fingers twining with hers, Laurie's eyes closed.

"Good." He worked his way to her jaw and down the side of her neck, where he scraped his teeth lightly along some magical cord there.

Robbed of speech by the hot shiver of current that raced through her, Laurie let her head fall sideways to give him better access. Anything, as long as he didn't stop.

He didn't stop. He slipped his arms around her and trailed his mouth around to the hollow of her throat.

Either the bed rose up to meet them, or Trey lowered her to the mattress, Laurie couldn't swear which. All she knew was that a moment later she was lying crossways on the comforter with Trey's solid, delicious weight anchoring her as he eased his thigh across hers.

With her hands free since he had released them, Laurie indulged her weeks-long fantasy and, mindful of his injuries, sank her fingers into his thick, black hair.

It wasn't soft, but neither was it coarse. It was full-bodied and luxurious, and she loved the feel of it against the sensitive skin between her fingers, the way it gleamed in the lamplight.

But there was more hair on his chest, and it drew her as if she were freezing and his chest promised warmth. "Off," she whispered, tugging his T-shirt up. "Help me."

The desperate rush in her voice sent heat pooling in Trey's loins. He wasn't alone here, neither in his bed nor in his wanting. He would give her whatever she asked for, everything she would take. She wanted his shirt off; it was gone. He whipped it over his head and tossed it somewhere behind him.

"Ah," she breathed.

Her hands on his chest felt like balm to a bruised soul. How was a man supposed to keep his head when a woman touched him this way?

The fleeting thought came to him that other women had touched him this way but it somehow hadn't felt the same, hadn't been as important. As life altering. And then he forgot them, those other women, because right here and now there was only Laurie. Here and now and tomorrow, for as many tomorrows as he could imagine, this was the woman he wanted touching him, the woman he wanted to touch.

Want. He wouldn't allow himself to think of need. Want, he could deal with. Need worried him, so he refused to consider it. He was too busy, anyway, just then to think straight as he fumbled the buttons free down the front of her blouse and kissed his way in their wake. Her skin was as sweet and soft as he had imagined it during the long, lonely nights of the past weeks. Tonight he wouldn't be lonely, but he prayed the hours with her in his arms would be long.

With the last of the buttons undone, he lifted her enough so he could pull the blouse free of her arms. Her bra was plain white cotton and, for some reason, sexy as hell. Then, in a heartbeat, it followed the way of her blouse and his T-shirt.

Now, he thought with a low growl. He shifted his weight until his chest pressed against her bare breasts and felt the breath leave his lungs. He could lie this

way forever, except he wanted his hands and mouth
on her breasts more than he wanted his next heartbeat.

He started at her mouth, kissing her, drinking the
soft moan from her lips. Then down her chin, her
throat, straight down to the silky, fragrant valley between those soft mounds that drew him like a siren's
call. He buried his face there and breathed in the es-
sence of her.

With his knee he nudged her legs apart and shifted
into the cradle of her thighs. And then he feasted,
trailing hot, wet kisses up the inner slope of one
breast, to the crest. With his tongue he flicked the
very tip.

"Ohh." Everything inside Laurie paused and
shifted, centering on that single spot where his tongue
teased her flesh. Pinpoints of heat and sensation, like
a sharp, electric current, made her arch her back.
When he closed his mouth over her nipple and suck-
led, she cried out in sheer pleasure. With both hands
she held his head there so he couldn't dare leave,
wouldn't dare stop tugging on that invisible wire that
led from his lips to her womb. She would gladly
spend the rest of her life lying on his bed with his
mouth at her breast and his weight between her
thighs.

Then he was moving, taking his mouth away, but
only to kiss his way to the other breast. Her whimper
of protest died half-born, and when he reached the
other nipple and thrust his hips against her, it became
a moan of tortured pleasure.

Never had she felt so much. Tingling heat and a
heaviness in her core, which seemed somehow both

empty and full. A lightness of weight, as if she would float off the mattress if Trey weren't holding her down. And emotions, so many emotions. Caring and gratitude, need and greed, a deep, hungry yearning. And something much stronger and deeper that she shied away from.

When his mouth left her breast and trailed up the side of her neck, Laurie pushed Trey onto his back, determined to give him back the pleasure she'd just received. And, in the process, she discovered that the pleasure had not been all hers. Hearing him suck in a sharp breath when she flicked her tongue over his nipple gave her a heady thrill. The knowledge that she could make this strong man moan helplessly by sucking on his nipple made her feel more powerful in her womanhood than she'd ever felt in her life.

No, the pleasure had not been all hers. If he had felt any of what she was now feeling, he had also been pleasuring himself. The thought thrilled her.

But soon Trey had had nearly all he could take of that particular torture. If she kept it up, he would likely lose control, and he wasn't ready to let the fire inside him burn them both just yet.

He turned the tables on her and rolled her to her back. It was time to rid her of her jeans, and he did so quickly.

He should have known, after seeing her bra, that her panties would also be plain white cotton. And they were. They were also bikinis, cut high enough on the sides to incite a man to riot. But they were in his way, keeping him from the treasure he sought. It was no problem to slide them down her shapely legs, no problem to follow them down with kisses clear to her toes.

Pale curls nestled at the juncture of her thighs. His hand went there with no need for direction from his mind, while he teased her navel with his tongue.

Laurie arched clear off the bed. She had to grab fistfuls of bedding to anchor herself. And then his mouth was on hers and his finger, only a single finger, slipped into that hot place that ached for him, and waves of sensation exploded deep inside her, radiating outward, taking her with them until there was nothing left of her but him.

Trey watched, humbled that he should be the man allowed to give this woman so much pleasure that her eyes became unfocused. He felt privileged in a way he never had before. And he'd waited as long as he could. But he waited longer still, until her gaze focused again. On him.

Shifting until his hips settled between hers, he pushed his way inside. Hot, damp velvet surrounded him like a glove.

Beneath him Laurie shifted and raised her knees to take more of him. He wanted to thank her for it, but words were beyond him. He could still feel the tiny pulses in the muscles surrounding him. He was literally feeling her pleasure. His control stretched wire thin.

With a final nudge of his hips, she took all of him. He wanted to stay there, just there, and never move again. But he had to move or go mad. Slowly at first an ancient, primitive rhythm took over, and he began to thrust, withdraw, thrust. And she was with him, gripping him with her knees, her arms around his neck, her hips rising in time with his.

Their harsh gasps for breath faded from his hearing as his blood roared in his ears and his loins.

He looked down at her and found her watching him. Their eyes met and held.

Laurie had never seen anything so stirring as the sight of Trey above her, his face taut with passion, his eyes nearly black with it.

And then she saw nothing as the world exploded in a whirl of colors, blinding her. She held on to him as the only solid thing in life, and let herself go.

When she cried out her release, Trey felt it all around him, and it was more than he could resist. Her flesh, her spirit called to him and took him straight over the edge of the world with her.

Laurie had no idea how long she lay there in Trey's arms, with his treasured weight on top of her. It might have been minutes, might have been hours. But when she was once again aware, she knew she was in for the heartache of her life. She was in love with Trey Wilder. Deeply, irrevocably in love.

But this was her problem, not his, and she vowed to keep it to herself. They had so little time left together, she did not want to spoil it. If he knew how she felt, he would likely become uncomfortable around her.

He wouldn't take a declaration of her love lightly, she was sure. He would feel responsible. And while he might be, simply because of the man he was, there was nothing he could do about it, unless he was willing to turn himself into a totally despicable person, one she could not possibly love.

And that was about as likely as pigs taking wing.

"Are we still alive?" he asked, his voice husky.

Laurie smiled against his shoulder. "Ask me again this time next week. I might have a coherent thought by then."

Deep laughter rumbled in his chest, vibrating clear through to hers.

Oh, the wonder of *feeling* his laughter. "I guess you must be all right. I don't think dead men laugh."

"Are you sure?"

"Pretty much."

When he raised himself onto his forearms and looked down at her, he was smiling. Then, as he gazed into her eyes, his smile faded. He traced a thumb along her cheek. "I think you've ruined me for other women."

Laurie felt a sudden tightening in her chest. She placed the fingers of one hand over his lips. "Don't say things like that. Don't look into the future."

Trey closed his eyes and tilted back his head. How easy it had been to forget, he thought. For the space of an hour he had set aside the fact that she had a job and a home and a life to go back to in less than three weeks.

Utah. What the hell was there in Utah that she couldn't find in Wyoming?

Whoa, pard. Was he actually thinking of asking her to stay? And do what? Live in his home and take care of his daughter? Be his housekeeper, *and, oh, by the way, we'll be sleeping together from now own, so get used to it?*

Trey wasn't sure where these thoughts were coming from, but he'd like to send them right back. He couldn't, wouldn't ask her for something as tacky as shacking up with him. That was damn sure no way for her to raise her daughters.

The obvious answer would be if they got—

Whoa. If he wasn't mistaken, the *M* word had been about to take residence in his brain. The very idea stunned him. Was he really thinking of getting married?

Well, hell, hadn't he been thinking that having Laurie and the girls in his home made him feel as if he had a family of his own?

Jeez, he was losing it. Marriage was about love and commitment. He could handle the commitment part, but they weren't in love with each other. He'd seen marriages like that and swore he'd never have anything to do with such a loveless, lifeless arrangement.

So what did that leave them?

Just under three weeks.

"Right," he said to her. "Better not to talk about the future." But that didn't mean he was ready to let her go. If he had so little time, he wanted to make the most of it. "This minute I'm thinking more about the past."

The look she gave him was filled with caution. "The past?"

"Yeah." He grinned and nudged his hips against hers, gratified at the way her eyes widened and darkened. "My teenage years. I'm feeling a lot like a randy teenager about now."

For Laurie the heartache had already begun. He had offered no argument at all about discussing the future. For them there was no such thing. At least, not in his mind. But for now he was in her arms, still, even, inside her body. She could feel him there, growing, hardening.

They still had this, she thought, and it was no small thing.

No small thing? She snickered at the mental pun.

"You think this is funny?" Trey said with feigned outrage.

"No, no," she protested as full laughter assailed her.

With a low growl he ran his hands up her ribs. "I'll give you something to laugh about, woman." He dug his fingers into her sides.

Laurie shrieked with laughter, squirming to get away from his tickling hands. Then her eyes widened, and she clamped a hand over her mouth. "Stop," she managed through breathless laughter. "Stop, you idiot, we'll wake the girls."

"Not me," he said innocently while dancing his fingers up her ribs. "I'm being real quiet. You're the one making all the noise."

Laurie solved the problem by pinching him on the rear.

"Hey, ow!"

"Now who's making all the noise."

A wicked gleam came into Trey's eyes. "I guess

we'll just have to think of something to keep ourselves quiet.''

Laurie felt the nudge of his hips. Her eyes slid shut, and she smiled in anticipation. ''What did you have in mind?''

''A little of this.'' He thrust slowly, all the way to the hilt.

Laurie's breath left in an audible *whoosh*.

''And a little of that.'' One fraction of an inch at a time, he withdrew. ''Then some more of this.'' By the time he thrust in again he was nearly breathless.

''I don't think,'' she managed, her own breathing becoming strained, ''that's going to keep me quiet.''

In. Out. In. ''It's not?''

''No.'' She tried to encourage him to move faster, but he gripped her hips and held her still. ''Any minute I might just scream, if you don't—'' Her voice trailed off on a moan.

''If I don't?''

''If you don't...move...faster.''

''I thought you'd never ask.''

Chapter Fourteen

The next day while Trey was over at headquarters, Donna came to see Laurie.

"This is a surprise," Laurie said. "Come in, come in."

Donna entered the house and, first things first, gave Carrie and Amy each a great big hug. Then she looked closely at Laurie. "My, don't you look chipper today."

"I do?" She knew she did. Looked chipper, felt chipper.

"Like the cat that swallowed the canary."

Laurie felt a blush sting her cheeks, but refused to acknowledge it.

Amy scrunched up her face. "A cat ate a canary?"

"It's just a figure of speech," Laurie told her.

Laurie could tell there was something on her aunt's

mind. The woman was positively about to burst, with what, Laurie couldn't guess. Donna kept sending a glance toward the girls, meaning she didn't want to talk in front of them.

Don't let it be trouble, Laurie silently pleaded. She was happy today. She didn't want to lose this warm, rosy glow that had surrounded her since she'd spent most of the night in Trey's bed. Even having to sneak back to her own room at three this morning like a naughty teenager hadn't dampened her spirits.

The only blot on her happiness was that she knew it was temporary and that at the end, when she left, she would be devastated. But that was later. This was now, and she didn't want to hear any bad news.

But Donna's eyes were twinkling just a little too much for whatever she had on her mind to be bad.

"I came over for two reasons," Donna said. "One, you left one of Katy's pacifiers over at the house Sunday."

"Oh, thanks, I've been wondering where that went. Of course, she's got nearly a dozen still in their packaging."

Donna laughed. "Trey had just bought out all the local stores, then we turned around and threw him a baby shower."

Laurie's grin stretched from ear to ear. "You threw Trey a baby shower? This I've got to hear."

"It's worth hearing, too. I could use a glass of tea if you want me to tell it right."

"Girls, Aunt Donna and I are going to have us a nice, long visit. Grown-up talk. Why don't you two go outside and play? Just remember, no—"

"No climbing trees," they said in unison.

"You got it." Laurie leaned down and kissed each one on the nose.

After the girls went out, Laurie poured a tall glass of iced tea for Donna and herself, and the two women settled where women tended to settle, at the kitchen table.

"Before we get into the baby shower, maybe you better spit out what you came here to tell me. You're about to burst with it."

"Tell you, nothing. *Ask* you, is more like it."

Laurie frowned. "Ask me what?"

"Okay, say it's none of my business, but it affects you, and it affects Trey, so that makes it my business twice over."

"What does?"

Donna laughed out loud. "I was going to ask you about the stupid grin Trey's been wearing since he showed up over at the house this morning. But since you've kinda got that same dazed look in your eyes, I guess I can figure things out for myself."

Heat flooded Laurie's cheeks. "I'm sure I don't know what you're talking about." Trey was wearing a stupid grin? The very thought made her smile.

"Oh, honey." Donna reached across the table and took Laurie's hand in hers. "I couldn't be happier. Nothing would please me more than to see you and the girls settle here with Trey. The two of you were made for each other."

The blood that had just flooded Laurie's cheeks now drained straight to her toes. "Aunt Donna, you've got it all wrong."

Donna's eyes widened. "Got what wrong? You're not going to try to convince me Trey's over there grinning like a fool because he likes the way you flip a pancake."

Laurie shook her head. The only words she could get out were, "I'm not staying, Aunt Donna. He... that is, we're not..." She stopped and blew out a breath. "What I'm trying to say is that in two and a half weeks, the girls and I will be going home, as planned."

"But why, when it's plain as the nose on your face that you're crazy about him."

Laurie blinked. "It is not."

"I saw that much on Sunday over at the house, with the two of you trying not to get caught staring at each other."

"We were doing no such thing."

Donna opened her mouth to respond, then snapped it shut. She eyed Laurie for a long moment before speaking. "All right, it's none of my business. But if you think he's not crazy about you, you're wrong. Looks to me like the two of you need to spend some time *out* of the bedroom, talking."

"Aunt Donna!"

"And I mean that in the nicest possible way," Donna said, grinning.

Laurie had loved and admired her aunt for too many years to take offense at her plain speaking, but talking wouldn't solve Laurie's problem.

"What if we did talk?" she asked. "What if you're right and he's crazy about me? That doesn't mean things would work out. How am I supposed to trust my judgment about men after Jimmy? How am I supposed to make a relationship work when I made such a mess of things before?''

''Now, that's enough of that kind of talk. I'll grant you didn't choose well the last time. Although Jimmy was good for one thing, bless his little pointed head—he sure sired good daughters. But that's about all he was good for. The only part of that divorce you were responsible for was way back when you said 'I do.' You just picked the wrong man, that's all. Trey is nothing like Jimmy. If you don't know that, you're not as smart as I always thought you were.''

''Of course he's not like Jimmy. But Aunt Donna, I'm still the same me, the same one who thought Jimmy hung the moon.''

''Oh, no.'' Donna shook her head. ''No, you're not. You were eighteen years old when you married him. A baby. You're older now and smarter.''

''God, I hope I'm smarter,'' Laurie muttered. ''I know I'm older. By about a million years.''

''You could always just apply for the job permanently,'' Donna said.

Laurie stared at her. ''Apply for what job?''

''This job, ninny. The job of Trey's housekeeper and nanny. That way you could stay, and whatever else came after that, well, at least you'd be here to let it happen.''

Laurie was shaking her head before Donna finished her sentence. ''Oh, no. I have a job, thank you, and a house. I've worked damn hard for both. And you want me to sweep floors for a living?''

''I happen to know you adore sweeping floors, and

these floors pay a darn sight more than teaching school. Think about it. Just promise me you'll think about it."

Donna left a short while later. Both of them forgot that she'd intended to tell Laurie about Trey's baby shower.

Laurie had very carefully sidestepped Donna's demand for a promise to think about the job as Trey's housekeeper, beyond her current agreement. She refused to think about it. There was no way she could stay, live in Trey's house, and not die a little bit each day knowing he didn't and probably never would return her love. It would kill her.

"Ho, ho, look at little brother," Jack said to Ace.

Trey had been cooling his heels in Ace's office for a half hour waiting for the two of them to show up. But he didn't mind leaning back in the big leather wingback chair, sipping coffee with his feet propped on Ace's desk. Gave him plenty of time to remember last night.

"I'd say he's feeling pretty chipper this morning," Ace said.

"I'm always chipper," Trey answered, smiling.

Jack laughed. "Not like this. Except now and then, and not at all lately."

Trey knew Jack expected him to take the bait. He just couldn't get worked up to being irritated with either of his brothers. It was too damn fine a day for irritation. Still, if he didn't respond, even halfheartedly, somebody would think he was sick and break out the thermometer.

"Okay," he said lazily. "I'll bite. What do you mean by that?"

"What he means," Ace said, his lips twitching, "is that you haven't looked this smug and happy since you came back from that weekend in Las Vegas. And now that we've all met Katy, we pretty much know what you did that weekend. Last night must have been a hell of a night."

Still half reclining, and with his feet propped on Ace's desk, Trey settled his coffee mug on his belly and leaned his head against the tall back of the chair. "Go ahead, try all you want. You can't make me mad today."

"Oh, ho," Jack said. "Does this mean she's staying?"

Trey narrowed his eyes. "Maybe I was wrong. Maybe you can make me mad. Butt out, bro. Both of you."

"Come on," Jack wheedled. For a grown man, he could wheedle like a champ. "It's us, number three. You can tell us."

"Do you talk about how you spend your nights with Lisa? Or you," he said to Ace, "with the fox?"

Ace narrowed his eyes. "I've told you before, that's my wife you're talking about."

"Yeah, and she's still a fox."

"Wait a minute," Jack said. "Listen to him, Ace. He's putting Laurie in with Lisa and Belinda. By God, he's in love with her."

Trey's feet hit the floor. Coffee sprayed across his chest and legs and the corner of Ace's desk.

"Hey, watch it," Ace protested.

"You watch it," Trey growled. "Nobody said any-thing about love, dammit." He wasn't in love. Of course he wasn't. What a damn fool thing for Jack to say.

Jack bit back a grin and rubbed his forefinger along the side of his nose. "Who was it who said something about protesting too much? Shakespeare?"

Trey glared at his brothers. "Who called this damn meeting, anyway? I've got work to do, even if the two of you don't."

"Okay." Ace held his hands up in surrender. "Backing off."

"For now," Jack added.

"We need to talk about the cattle rustling," Ace said.

All personal matters flew out the door. This was ranch business, and it was serious.

"What's the latest word?" Trey asked.

"Dane says they're getting bolder, taking more cat-tle each time they hit. If they stick to their current pattern, they'll hit Wyatt County in the next few weeks. We need to be ready."

"Patrols?" Trey asked.

"That's what I'm thinking."

They got down to business and made what plans they could. The herd was currently on the government lease land up in the mountains. The rustlers wouldn't be able to get up there with the truck and trailer it was suspected they used, but there was nothing to keep them from cutting out however many cattle they wanted and herding them down on horseback.

"So that's our first priority," Ace said. "We'll send riders up there to keep an eye on things."

They talked for another thirty minutes, covering every angle they could think of, using what little information the sheriff had been able to pass along to Ace.

By the time Trey left for home it was nearly lunchtime, and he was in a foul mood. Thinking about cattle rustlers would do that to a rancher, but most of his irritability came from Jack's crack about Trey being in love with Laurie.

Of course he wasn't in love with her.

In lust, yeah. He would have to admit that—but not to his brothers, by damn.

He liked her, certainly. Respected and admired her. Adored her daughters. And the thought of them leaving in a couple of weeks left him feeling as if he were staring into a gaping black tunnel that was his future.

But that wasn't love. He'd been there, done that and had the scars to prove it. He wasn't any good at love, and if he was going to be honest with himself, the thought of opening up to Laurie and taking the chance that she didn't return his feelings left his stomach in icy knots.

No way. He wouldn't do that to himself again.

He supposed it was perverse of him that when he got home for lunch, he was almost glad Laurie didn't seem to be in any better mood than he was.

Nothing much seemed to have changed by the time supper rolled around. She didn't seem angry. She was fine with the girls. But she wouldn't look at him. Not in the eye. He wondered why, but figured maybe he was better off not knowing.

Coward.

Yeah, well…maybe.

Yet, despite his own inner demons and whatever was eating at Laurie, they ended up together in Katy's room after Carrie and Amy went to bed.

"I'm just changing her," Laurie said when he stopped in the doorway.

"Way to go, sweet pea," Trey said to his daughter. "I just changed you a half hour ago, now you're making Laurie do it."

"Yeah, well," Laurie said. "Just tell your daddy that that's what babies are supposed to do."

"Supposed to?" Trey asked, feeling some of the tension of the day ease out of his shoulders. Part of the easing, he knew, was caused by being with Katy. But another part was Laurie. He wondered what that meant.

"Of course, Daddy," Laurie said on Katy's behalf. "Say, that's my job. I'm supposed to go through as many diapers as I can before you potty train me. It's a rule."

"A rule, huh?"

"Yep. A baby rule. There you go, young lady." Laurie stuck the last tab in place, then rearranged Katy's pajamas. "All set to say good night?"

Katy's answer was a big yawn.

Trey grinned. "That's my girl."

"Obedient little thing, isn't she," Laurie said.

Laurie turned to leave, while Trey kissed his daughter good-night. "Sweet dreams, sweet pea."

He wondered, when he stepped into the living room, if Laurie would be there, of if she had gone on to bed. Alone.

She was there. Just standing there in the middle of the room, with her back to him. Waiting for him? He hoped so.

"Laurie?"

She turned, and for the first time since that morning, when he'd left her with a blistering kiss, she looked him in the eye.

He couldn't ask. He didn't have the words. So instead, he simply held out his hand and uttered a silent prayer that she would know how much he wanted her. That she wouldn't notice his hand wasn't quite steady.

When he held out his hand, Laurie nearly sagged with relief. He'd been so distant tonight—but then, so had she, she admitted—that she'd wondered if he would want her again. The slight tremor in his hand and the question in his eyes gave her the answer she needed. She took his hand and walked with him down the hall to his bed.

They made love that night, and the nights that followed, with an intensity bordering on desperation. Each time they came together, it was as if they knew their time was running out and they were trying to hold on to this magic for as long as they could.

But they never talked about it. They simply held on to each other as tightly as possible during the night, and went on about their business during the day.

Every night Trey could feel her slipping a little bit

farther away from him, as if her mind had already turned toward Utah.

"Dammit all to hell." He was in the shed making some adjustments to the bailer he would use next week after he swathed the alfalfa and let it cure. At the thought of Laurie going back to Utah, he swore and threw his wrench at the wall.

She was really going to do it. She was really going to just pack up and leave at the end of next week. Never mind that he still needed her to take care of Katy. Never mind that he still wanted her, desperately.

He could offer her the job permanently. The thought had danced around in his head a time or two lately. But would she take it?

Why should she? She had that teaching job that started soon. She must have worked damn hard for her teaching degree, going to college while raising two little girls. And they were about to move into their first house, right near the school where she would teach and her girls would attend classes. She was supposed to give that up for him?

He tried to put himself in her place, but found he couldn't. Not really. He didn't know how a woman would feel about living with a man not her husband, raising her daughters in his house. Would people in town talk? Would she care if they did?

He would care, dammit. He didn't want people saying bad things about her, didn't want Carrie and Amy gossiped about.

And what if she did stay, and what if some man came along and asked her to marry him?

There it was, the *M* word.

Trey picked up a screwdriver and sent it the way of the wrench.

By damn, if there was going to be any marrying going on around here, it was going to be him and—

Good God. That was it. That was the answer. They could get married.

Oh, yeah, like she's going to say yes to you?

Well, why wouldn't she? She must care about him or she wouldn't come so willingly to his bed every night, wouldn't respond so sweetly and fiercely in his arms.

And she liked him well enough, didn't she? And the girls, well, he just plain adored them, and he figured they liked him okay. They'd been living as a family, all of them, for weeks. Why should that stop?

From across the yard he heard the girls laughing, taking turns in the swing he'd hung for them in the old elm, to give them something to do around the tree besides climb it.

Laurie must be in the house.

With a rag from his hip pocket, he started wiping the grease off his fingers and strode toward the back-door.

He found her in the living room. She was seated in the rocker, feeding Katy.

"How's she doing?" he asked.

"Gobbling it up, as usual," Laurie said. "She's growing like a weed, this girl is."

"Yeah, I know." He dragged the ottoman over and sat down and watched his daughter nurse from her bottle.

"Something on your mind?" Laurie asked.

Trey wiped his palms down the thighs of his jeans. "Yeah. There is."

"She'll be through in a few minutes, if you want to wait until I put her down."

"No, that's okay. I can talk while she eats." This was better, Trey thought. This way, with her arms full of baby, she couldn't easily throw something at him if he messed this up and it came out all wrong.

Laurie cocked her head. "Trey, what is it?"

He pulled the ball cap from his head and stared at it for a long minute before looking back at her. "I've got a proposition for you."

Chapter Fifteen

"This sounds serious," Laurie said. In fact, he looked serious. Nerves started dancing along her spine.

"It is." He fiddled with his hat again. "And I want you to hear me out before you answer."

Now he was starting to worry her. "All right."

He rested his forearms on his thighs and let the hat dangle between his knees. He turned it this way, then that way, studying it as if it contained the answers to world hunger.

"You're going home soon," he finally said.

Laurie felt her chest tighten. "That's right."

He looked up at her. "What if you don't?"

She blinked. "What do you mean?"

"You could stay, you know. I don't mean as my housekeeper. That wouldn't work for long. There'd be too much talk about you and the girls living with me, and I don't want that for you or Carrie and Amy.''

Laurie's mouth dried out. "No. That wouldn't be good for any of us.''

"We could get married.''

Laurie feared very much that she'd lost the thread of the conversation. She could have sworn he'd just said— "What?''

"You know, the *M* word. Married.''

She opened her mouth, but nothing came out.

"Hear me out before you say anything,'' he said in a rush. "Look, I know we're not madly in love with each other or anything.''

Something cold and hard settled in the pit of Laurie's stomach. She thought maybe it was what was left of her heart.

"But we've both been in love before, and it was a disaster, right? We like each other, respect each other, and God knows I worship Carrie and Amy like they were my own. I'd be willing to have more children if you were.''

Again her mouth opened. She had to stop this madness somehow. But her voice refused to work.

"Your daughters need a full-time father, Laurie, and Katy needs a mother. I don't mean that's the only reason we should get married, but it's something to think about. And we're good together, you and I. Even out of bed,'' he added with a crooked smile. "But in bed, I told you the first time we made love that you've spoiled me for other women. I wasn't joking. And no,'' he said holding up his hand, "I don't think we should get married just so we can sleep together. It's all of it, don't you see? Us, the kids, we'd be a family. There's a hole in my life every bit as big as the hole in yours. We could fill that for each other. So that's my proposition. That we get married.''

"Trey, I—"

"No." Trey held up a hand to stop her. He couldn't let her answer him yet. "Don't say anything right now." He could see in her eyes that if she answered now, she would say no. "Just think about it. You said you'd think about it."

He could see something else in her eyes, too. It was tears, gathering and getting ready to overflow, and if they did it would tear him to pieces.

He pushed himself to his feet. "I'm going back out to the shed. See you at supper."

Laurie gaped at his back as he walked away. See you at supper? *See you at supper?* He just turned her entire world upside down, and he'd *see her at supper?*

She let her head fall against the back of the rocker and closed her eyes, feeling the tears slide down her cheeks. "Katy, what am I going to do about that daddy of yours? He knew I was about to cry. The coward took off, that's what he did."

And if she thought about it for half a second, she was grateful.

Married. He thought they should get married. And if it wasn't the oddest marriage proposal she'd ever heard of, she didn't know what was.

But he was being honest with her. That was his way. He could easily have told her he loved her, and she would have fallen all over him. She wondered if he knew that.

God, she hoped not. She hoped the secrets of her heart were safe from those brilliant blue eyes.

He wanted them to get married. He'd been serious. She didn't know whether to laugh or cry—she'd just done that, hadn't she?—or scream and throw something pricey and breakable.

What he wanted was a companion, sex, hot meals and a baby-sitter.

"Katy," she said, sniffing the last of her tears away, "your daddy is a jerk."

Laurie did her best to nurse her irritation and outrage, although privately, throughout the afternoon and evening. The alternative was to curl up into a tight ball of pain and weep her eyes out.

I know we're not madly in love with each other or anything.

"Speak for yourself," she muttered.

"Did you say something, Mama?"

"What, Carrie? Oh. No. Just talking to myself." *And I'd better stop it.* She'd been so involved with her own problems she'd completely forgotten for a moment that it was time for supper and the girls were setting the table.

Somehow they made it through the meal. Laurie was even able to eat, although why she didn't choke on her food she didn't know. Her throat was so tight it was a wonder that anything went down.

I know we're not madly in love with each other or anything.

Those words kept playing over and over in her head like the refrain of a well-known song.

After the girls were asleep and Katy was down for the night, Laurie wanted to curl up in her bed alone and cry herself to sleep. But Trey stood there in the hall, waiting for her, holding out his hand. She wanted him so much, loved him so much, that she didn't know which would hurt more, to walk away or to go with him to his bed.

"I didn't mean to make you angry," he said quietly. "I just thought...hell, Laurie, the way you give yourself to me every night, you have to care something for me, don't you?"

Care for him? She nearly laughed. *Care* was such a pale word for what she felt. But could she spend the rest of her life with a man who didn't love her and perhaps never would? And the more immediate question, could she spend another night in his arms?

She wanted so much more for them than to simply fill a need in each other's lives. More than to provide a family for their children. More than to ease the terrible loneliness she had lived with for longer than she cared to remember.

She wanted him to love her. Wanted to be able to trust him, rely on him, give herself to him completely, body, heart and soul, and know that her trust was well placed and returned. She wanted to bask confidently in the love of the man she cherished.

"Come." Trey spoke gently and took her by the hand. He could see the struggle on her face, and it ate at him. She must care for him or her decision wouldn't be this hard on her. So if she cared for him,

what was holding her back? "Sit with me and talk."
He led her toward his room, but for once he didn't
have sex on his mind. Other parts of his body would
just have to wait.

"Talk?" she asked.

"Talk." In his room he closed the door and pulled
her over to the bed. He sat and piled the pillows up
behind him and pulled her down to rest in his arms.
"Tell me what hurts so much."

"What makes you think anything hurts?"

"Honey." He used one finger beneath her chin to
turn her face up to his. "You should see your face.
You look like your best friend just died. Since you
were fine before I asked you to marry me, I have to
figure that's causing you a problem."

"You don't really want to get married, do you."
She made it a statement rather than a question.

"I thought I didn't. I came close once, and after
that didn't work out, I just figured marriage wasn't
for me."

"Do you realize that's the most personal thing
you've ever told me about yourself?"

"It is?" He shrugged. "I don't talk much about
myself."

"Not even to the woman you say you want to
marry?"

She had him there. "Good point. Okay, what do
you want to know?"

"I've learned more about you from people at the
grocery store in town than I have from you."

Trey narrowed his eyes. "What people?"

"Mrs. Biddle, for one."

He chuckled. "I suppose she told you about the time I used my mother's lipstick to draw a pair of big red lips on all the grapefruit."

"No, actually, she only told me about the trail of croutons you left. But I was supposed to ask you about the grapefruit. She'll be proud that you confessed."

"All right, so you've heard about my misspent youth. What else do you want to know about?"

Her gaze lowered, flicked up, then away. "Cindy."

That one took him by surprise. A nasty surprise. "Where'd you hear that name?"

"That's what Dane called the tall redhead who accosted me in Biddle's the other day."

"Accosted you?" He sat up straight and nearly dumped her off the bed. "What do you mean, accosted you? If that—"

"It was nothing physical, and I took care of it. But she informed me in no uncertain terms that…something about my never getting my hooks in you, or something. She said I'd never get you to marry me."

"Won't she be surprised."

"Don't change the subject."

"I'm not."

"Who is she to you, Trey?"

He let out a long breath. "Okay. I'm not very good at this communication stuff. Cindy and I dated for a while."

"She indicated it was a lot more than that."

"I'm getting to it. We dated, and, jeez, this is embarrassing. I fell for her, okay? We decided to get

married. Everything was going fine until about a
month before the wedding when she started talking
about places like Las Vegas and Acapulco and New
York. I figured, sure, we could probably visit one of
those places a year.''

''Ah.''

''Ah?''

''Never mind. Keep going.''

''Well, it turned out that she didn't want to visit
those places, she wanted to live in one or more of
them. Expected me to sell my share of the ranch.
Somewhere she got the idea that if I did, we'd have
enough money to live on—in style—for the rest of
our lives.''

''And you said no.''

''I said no.'' Suddenly alarmed, he leaned sideways
and looked at her. ''Is that part of what's bothering
you? You don't want to live out here in the middle
of nowhere? Damn.'' He sat up and buried his face
in his hands. ''I hadn't thought of that. Damn.''

''Trey, no. The ranch is not a problem. I love it
here, you must know that.''

''You do?''

''Of course I do. So do the girls.''

Trey let out a sigh of relief and lay down again,
pulling her back against his side. In about a year his
heart rate might settle down to normal. He didn't even
want to consider what he might have done if Laurie
hadn't wanted to live on the Flying Ace.

''Okay,'' he said. ''It's your turn.''

''My turn to what?''

''To tell me your deepest, darkest secret.''

"Are you saying that Cindy was your deepest, darkest secret? I don't buy it."

"Not Cindy, exactly. But she's part of it. Mainly it's that I'd just about rather have my arms and legs amputated than live anywhere but the Flying Ace. Is that dark enough for you?"

Laurie slipped her arm around his waist. He'd said it in a lazy manner, but she'd heard the underlying pain he'd tried to disguise. This land was everything to him. How could that woman ever have thought he would leave?

"Yes," she told him. "That's more than dark enough. Any other women I should watch out for in town?"

He chuckled, as she'd meant him to. "Not that I know of. After Cindy, I pretty much swore off women for a while. No offense, but they're damn untrustworthy creatures, present company excepted, of course."

"You think I'm trustworthy?"

"Yeah," he said quietly. "Yeah, I do. And you know what? It feels good, trusting you. After Cindy, then Katy's mother, I'd about decided women weren't worth the trouble."

"Katy's mother?"

"I thought Donna told you about her."

Laurie shook her head. "Just that she decided she didn't want to raise the baby, so she sent her here to you."

"If it was that simple I wouldn't be wrestling over what to tell Katy someday when she's older. No, Katy's mother didn't want to raise a baby. That much was true. In fact, she decided before Katy was born to put her up for adoption. Only after the deal fell through at the last minute did she decide to let me know I was a father.''

''But that's not right.''

''No kidding.'' He jostled her with his arm. ''Now it's your turn. Come on, lady, talk.''

''I don't know what to say. I don't really have any secrets.''

''There's not a woman alive who doesn't have secrets. You'll never get me to believe otherwise. Tell me why you don't want to marry me.''

He slipped that last sentence in smooth as silk and took her by surprise. ''I haven't decided that I don't want to. You asked me to think about it, and I'm still thinking.''

''What makes it so hard to decide?''

Dear God, what should she tell him? That it was hard because she was in love with him and he didn't love her?

Heaven help her, she couldn't tell him that. She rolled away from him and sat cross-legged next to his hip, facing the foot of the bed so he couldn't see her face. ''This is hard.''

''Why?'' Trey asked. ''After the past week or so that we've spent together in this bed, I wouldn't think there was much of anything we couldn't say to each other.''

''The things you've told me tonight…they're important, and I'm glad you told me. But they're basically over with. In the past. Mine isn't.''

''Your what isn't?''

She shrugged. "My problem. My secret. You know how you said you don't trust women?"

"You don't trust men?"

"I guess." She shrugged again, feeling a blush stain her cheeks. She was glad he couldn't see. "Sort of. But really it's myself I don't trust."

"I trust you."

"So you said. But you're not counting on me to make a better choice this time, to make it work this time."

Behind her, he was quiet for a moment. Then he said. "Aren't I? If I do say so myself, I think I'm a better choice than your ex, and if you marry me, it wouldn't just be you who had to make it work, it would be both of us."

"Why do you have to make it sound so...so right? So good? So...possible?"

"Because it's all those things."

"No." She swung around and faced him. "No, Trey, it's not. It's...it's cold, calculated. It's like a business deal or something."

"Cold? How can you sit on this bed and even think the word? Oh, I get it. You mean the *L* word."

She laughed sadly and shook her head. "Poor Trey. Is it so bad a word that you can't even say it?"

This time it was his turn to shrug. "Love. There. Satisfied? It's just not something I trust. It doesn't last. Not the man-woman kind of love, anyway."

"How can you say that?" she cried.

"Easy. Look around. Who do you know who's still in love after a few years?"

"What about your brothers and their wives? Your

sister and her husband? They're all in love. You can see it in their faces."

He waved a hand in the air as if to negate her suggestion. "They're all still newlyweds."

"My parents. They've been married nearly thirty years."

Trey turned his gaze toward the ceiling. "Yeah, let's see. These would be the same parents whose home you left a few weeks ago because they fought all the time? If that's love, you can count me out. Give me things like honor and commitment any day. Those are things a person can control. Love's too messy."

"Then I'm sorry for you, Trey, because I disagree." She slid to the side of the bed and stood. "To me love is the most important thing on earth."

"Laurie, wait," he called as she walked to the door.

Before leaving she turned back and looked at him. "Good night. I'm going to bed."

His face was stiff and tight, but his voice was soft. "Does this mean you've made up your mind?"

"I don't know," she said. "I'm going to sleep on it."

But they both feared she was lying. She believed too strongly in love to settle for anything less.

Chapter Sixteen

Laurie's eyes were hot and dry as she lay awake that night and stared at the dark ceiling above her bed. Her emotions and her logic were at war with each other. For that matter her differing emotions were having their own battle that had not much at all to do with logic.

She couldn't believe she was even considering Trey's...what had he called it? A proposition. Not a proposal.

It was her heart that was doing the considering, because it was her heart that wanted so very badly to stay with him, to love him, to be loved by him.

But Trey didn't love her. He probably never would.

Oh, he cared for her, she knew that, or he wouldn't be asking to share the rest of his life with her.

Yes, her heart wanted to say, but that fickle organ

was also terrified of being crushed by his indifference toward love.

Around and around her emotions circled each other. Yearning, longing, love. Uncertainty. Fear.

Perhaps she should try logic again. If she married him, he got everything he wanted: a family of his own, a mother for his daughter, a cook, a house-keeper, a lover.

For her part, Laurie would not get the one thing she wanted most, and that was love.

But she would get a wonderful father for Carrie and Amy. She would get to call Katy her own, with the chance for more children if she wanted them. She got a lovely home in the middle of wide-open spaces that enthralled her. She got to be the one thing she'd always wanted to be, a full-time homemaker. And she got the best, tenderest, most exciting lover a woman could ask for.

There was only one thing she didn't get. Could she live without the love she wanted?

Why not? You never planned to fall in love and remarry.

That was true. After her divorce she had faced the fact that she might well spend the rest of her life as a single, unattached woman, and the thought had not troubled her much.

So what was the problem if she got all those other things, without something she hadn't expected any-way?

But she knew the problem. It was living day in and day out with a man she loved, knowing he didn't return her feelings.

How long before the pain of it crippled her? How long before she grew to resent his lack of feelings? With resentment came bitterness and the destruction of trust. Because of her love for him, she could easily destroy whatever they might manage to build together.

Perhaps, she thought wearily, a clean break would be the best. For her, at least. Trey would find someone to hire, and if he didn't, Donna and his family were nearby.

Yet to never see him again, never hear his laugh, never taste his smile…never see little Katy grow into the beautiful woman she would one day become… To spend the rest of her life without feeling Trey's strong arms around her in the night. How could she live like that?

Then again…

What Laurie had to decide was which would hurt less—a clean break and a return to Utah, or the slow torture of living with a man who didn't love her?

God help her, what was she going to do?

By morning Laurie realized she had known all along that she couldn't marry Trey if he didn't love her. She just hadn't had the courage to admit it. Or the honesty.

But when she saw the wary look in Trey's eyes, mixed ever so faintly with hope, she kept her decision to herself. For some small spark of hope was still alive inside her, too. Hope that some miraculous answer to the problem would suddenly appear. An answer that would let her stay with Trey without the terrible risk of having her heart ripped out. An answer that would make Trey fall in love with her.

But no such miraculous answer appeared over bacon and eggs that morning.

But one did appear—or rather, call—about mid-morning. It might not have been the one she would have wanted, but it forced her to admit something she hadn't previously considered. Trey might like and respect her, as he'd said. He might want her. But he did not need her. Not *her*, Laurie Oliver.

All he really needed was someone to take care of his daughter and his home. If he wanted a wife, he was going to have to go out and find one, rather than take the easy, convenient way out by marrying her because she happened to be handy.

Oh, damn, she didn't want to be angry with him. She was too confused and dispirited to be angry.

Her miraculous answer came via the telephone, with one simple declaration: "I'm calling about the ad for housekeeper and nanny."

Her name was Mary Cunningham. She was fifty-seven years old, from Cheyenne, a widow and retired pediatric nurse. She loved children, the country life and taking care of a home. She was willing to relocate, and available to start work next week.

She sounded, in a word, perfect.

A miraculous answer.

Laurie wrote down the woman's phone number and promised to have Trey call her back.

She could lose the number. The thought blazed in her mind between laundry and vacuuming. She could call the woman back herself and tell her the job was filled, then tell Trey she would marry him. He would never know that he'd had a real choice.

But *she* would know and would never be able to live with the lie.

She stood in the living room and looked around. Two coloring books and a box of crayons rested on the coffee table, and the serape draped across Trey's recliner needed folding. Otherwise the room was neat. It was a good room.

It was a good house, she thought as she wandered from room to room. From outside in the backyard came the sound of her daughters' laughter. Such a happy, healthy sound, and so much easier and more frequent than it had ever been before.

But there would be plenty of laughter in their new home, she promised herself. She would see to it. Just because her heart would be in pieces, strewn across the Wyoming rangeland, didn't mean she couldn't give her girls all the love and security they deserved.

She would be going home to a new house, a new job, a new life. That was something, wasn't it?

And you'll never see Trey again.

Dear God, how would she stand it? How was it possible to care so deeply, to love so strongly, when she'd known him only a few weeks?

How was it possible that she could hurt this much?

But the truth would not be avoided. He didn't love her, and now he didn't even need her.

Blindly she lowered herself to the smooth, wooden rocker where she had spent so many hours holding Katy. It was time to face the truth. It was time for her and her girls to go home.

* * *

When Trey found her there sometime later he knew instantly that something was wrong.

He'd come to the house to use the phone. The damn tire was already low again on the tractor. He did not want to have to deal with airing it up every couple of hours when he started on the alfalfa next week. He needed to call around and see if anyone had a replacement in stock.

To see Laurie sitting idly in the rocker, staring off into space, when he'd never seen her motionless before, stunned him. Worried him. She was always busy, always cleaning this or rearranging that, and usually smiling while she did it. She was seldom, if ever, idle.

"Laurie?" He knelt before her. "Laurie, what's wrong?"

Slowly she turned her head toward him. "What?" She blinked, and her gaze finally focused on him. "Oh. Trey."

Trey had seen a man in shock once. He'd worn the same confused glaze in his eyes as he saw in Laurie's now. "Laurie, talk to me. Tell me what's wrong."

"Wrong?" She blinked again. "Oh. I, uh, I wrote it down. It's next to the phone in the kitchen."

"Wrote what down?"

"The phone number."

"What phone number? Is somebody hurt? Ace? Jack?"

"No. No, I'm sorry. I didn't mean to worry you. It's Mary Cunningham's phone number."

"All right," Trey said slowly. "Who is Mary Cunningham?"

Suddenly Laurie's eyes cleared and she truly looked at him for the first time since he'd come in. "She's the woman you're going to hire so you don't need to marry me."

Trey sat abruptly on his heels. His stomach tightened. His mouth dried out. "What?" He didn't know why he was so surprised. Ever since she walked out of his room last night he'd feared this moment was coming. But now, in addition to everything else, he was confused. "Who is she?"

"She's perfect, Trey. Exactly what you want and need. She's a fifty-seven-year-old retired pediatrics nurse, widowed, willing to relocate, loves the country and can start work next week. So you see, you don't need to marry me now. The girls and I will go home as planned."

Trey stared at her for a long minute, searching for the words to change her mind, to make her see what a mistake she was making, for both of them. The words did not come out as planned.

"You think I want to marry you so I don't have to hire a damn housekeeper?" he roared.

"Well, no, not exactly."

"I want to marry you because this is where you belong, dammit." The words still weren't the right ones, he knew, but at least he wasn't yelling now. "You and Carrie and Amy, here with Katy and me. I can't believe everything we've shared means so little to you that you can just walk out. What the hell's so great about Utah? Why do you want to take the girls and go back there?"

"No!" wailed two young voices from the back-door.

Ah, hell, Trey thought. He hadn't meant for Carrie and Amy to hear any of this.

"We can't go home, Mama," Amy cried. "Mr. Trey needs us. Don't you, Mr. Trey? And so does Katy."

"Amy's right, Mama," Carrie said, her eyes filled with sudden tears. "We don't wanna go home. We wanna stay here."

Laurie's heart ached for the distress on her daughters' faces. She wished desperately that she could spare them this pain. "We don't live here, girls, you know that. This isn't our home."

"But it could be," Carrie said desperately. Carrie, who so seldom let her emotions show. "Couldn't it, Mr. Trey."

Both girls sidled up to him and looked accusingly at their mother.

Trey put his arms around them and hugged them to his sides. "Tell you what, girls. Why don't you go back outside and play and let me talk to your mother about this." He had never told them to do anything before. He was probably stepping all over Laurie's motherhood toes, but he was a desperate man. They had helped his cause, he hoped, but he didn't want them caught in the middle between him and their mother.

"Trey's right, girls," Laurie said. God, her face was pale. Even her lips looked bloodless. "Go back out and play and let us talk about it."

"But we want to stay," Carrie said, her speech

more controlled now. "We want to stay here and live here. Mr. Trey wants us to, don't you, Mr. Trey?"

Well, hell, he thought. That was neatly done. Carrie had just taken herself and her sister out of the middle and stuck him there. "What I want right now," he answered carefully, "is to talk to your mother. Will you go outside and play so I can do that?"

"Will you talk her into staying here?" Amy asked in the most pitiful voice he'd ever heard.

"I don't know, honey. It's not that simple. Let us talk about it, okay?"

"Oh, okay," she said with a sniff.

With obvious reluctance, and three pauses to look back over their shoulders, Carrie and Amy went back outside.

Trey sagged with relief.

Laurie dropped her head to the back of the chair and closed her eyes. "Thank you for that."

"For what?"

"For not using them against me."

"Don't think I wasn't tempted," he said ruefully. "But you heard them, Laurie. They want to stay."

"Trey—"

"You said I didn't need you now that this woman has called. You're partly right." He rose to his knees and took her hands in his. "I don't need you to cook and clean and change Katy's diapers and feed her. I can hire somebody to do those things."

"That was your plan all along."

"But that doesn't mean I don't need you." Somehow it didn't bother him at all to admit his need. "I need you beside me, facing the days with me, and the nights. I need you there with me to watch Katy grow up, and I need to be beside you for Carrie and Amy. Don't go, Laurie. For God's sake, don't leave me. If you don't want to get married right away, I'll wait until you do. Just *don't leave me.*''

Laurie gazed at him in wonder, her heart racing in her chest. He couldn't know how much his words meant to her. She wondered if he understood what his words meant, period. ''But, Trey, you said you didn't love me.''

''No, I said I didn't trust love, and I don't. It scares the hell out of me. I don't know if that's what I feel for you. All I know is I want you and I need you in a way I've never wanted or needed another living soul. If you don't love me, give us a chance. Maybe it will come in time. I know I'm not the most open guy around, but if you want me to spill my guts, I'll talk about myself until you're sick of hearing it. I swear to you I'll never lie to you or betray you in any way. Stay with me, Laurie. Be my wife. We can make it work, whatever it takes. I know we can.''

Her vision dimmed. She had to blink to clear away the flood of tears in her eyes. ''I don't believe any woman has ever heard a more beautiful declaration of love than what you just gave me.''

''If that's love, then I've got a never-ending supply inside me for you. Marry me, Laurie. Say yes.''

With a sob of joyful surrender, she slid from the chair into his arms. ''Oh, yes. Yes, yes, yes.''

Trey closed his eyes and held her as tightly as he dared. ''Thank God.''

Epilogue

Two Years Later

Anyone driving along the north side of the Flying Ace Ranch that Tuesday afternoon would have seen Trey Wilder out standing in his field.

He stood with his hands on his hips, surrounded by one of the best stands of alfalfa anyone in Wyatt County had seen in years. He was outstanding in his field, if he did say so himself.

The feeling of satisfaction that filled him had been with him for two years now, and very little of it had to do with crop production, and everything to do with the cause of that rooster tail of dust coming down the road toward the house.

They're home.

With a shout and a wave, he left the alfalfa in a

hurry and met the car as it turned into the driveway. As soon as it stopped, girls tumbled out. Three of them, and they were all his. Carrie, Amy and two-year-old Katy ran to him.

"We're home, Daddy," Amy cried.

"Did you miss us?" Carrie wanted to know.

"Hungry." Katy liked one-word sentences, and she liked her food on demand.

Another female climbed out of the vehicle. She was the other half of his heart, this wife of his. Then Laurie Wilder placed her bundle in his arms and grinned.

"She's all yours now, Daddy, and she needs changing."

Trey looked down into the face of their youngest daughter. "Her three-month checkup went okay?"

"She's the picture of health."

"We knew that, didn't we, sweet Sara?"

Trey leaned over the baby and gave his wife a slow, deep kiss. "Have I told you today I love you?"

"No," Laurie said, her green eyes twinkling. "Why don't you?"

Trey kissed her again. "I love you."

"There they go again," Carrie said in the bored tone she'd recently acquired, now that she was an older woman of eight. "Come on, girls, let's go find something to eat. A person would starve around here waiting on those two to stop kissing."

"Kiss me, Mama, kiss me." There were some multiword sentences Katy could manage just fine, and that was one of her favorites.

Trey rested his forehead against Laurie's. Never

had a man been blessed with so many treasures, and he was deeply grateful for each and every one.

And it didn't hurt anything that he was the only man in a houseful of females. Every man should be so blessed.

*   *   *   *   *

**Coming soon from
Silhouette Special Edition™:
The continuation of a popular series**

MONTANA MAVERICKS

**With brand-new titles from
three exciting authors:**

CHRISTMAS IN WHITEHORN
by Susan Mallery
(SE #1435, on sale December 2001)

IN LOVE WITH HER BOSS
by Christie Ridgway
(SE #1441, on sale January 2002)

MARKED FOR MARRIAGE
by Jackie Merritt
(SE #1447, on sale February 2002)

*Come home to Whitehorn, Montana,
and celebrate family togetherness
and true love this holiday season!*

Silhouette®
Where love comes alive™

THE FORTUNES OF TEXAS

invite you to a memorable Christmas celebration in

Gifts of

FORTUNE

Patriarch Ryan Fortune has met death head-on and now he has a special gift for each of the four honorable individuals who stood by him in his hour of need. This holiday collection contains stories by three of your most beloved authors.

THE HOLIDAY HEIR
by Barbara Boswell

THE CHRISTMAS HOUSE
by Jennifer Greene

MAGGIE'S MIRACLE
by Jackie Merritt

And be sure to watch for **Did You Say Twins?!** by Maureen Child, the exciting conclusion to the *Fortunes of Texas: The Lost Heirs* miniseries, coming only to Silhouette Desire in December 2001.

Don't miss these unforgettable romances... available at your favorite retail outlet.

Silhouette®
Where love comes alive™

Celebrate the season with

Midnight Clear

A holiday anthology featuring
a classic Christmas story from
New York Times bestselling author

Debbie Macomber

Plus a brand-new *Morgan's Mercenaries* story
from *USA Today* bestselling author

Lindsay McKenna

And a brand-new *Twins on the Doorstep* story
from national bestselling author

Stella Bagwell

Available at your favorite retail outlets in November 2001!

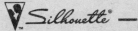